④ ⑥/94

The Hobbema Prospect

by the same author

Superintendent Kenworthy novels

CORRIDORS OF GUILT
THE ASKING PRICE
THE SUNSET LAW
THE GREEN FRONTIER
SURRENDER VALUE
PLAYGROUND OF DEATH
THE ANATHEMA STONE
SOME RUN CROOKED
NO BIRDS SANG
HANGMAN'S TIDE
DEATH IN MIDWINTER
DEATH OF AN ALDERMAN

Inspector Brunt novels

MR FRED
DEAD-NETTLE
GAMEKEEPER'S GALLOWS
RESCUE FROM THE ROSE

non-fiction

THE LANGUAGE LABORATORY IN SCHOOL
LANGUAGE TEACHING: A SYSTEMS APPROACH

JOHN BUXTON HILTON

The Hobbema Prospect

A Superintendent Kenworthy novel

St. Martin's Press
New York

Library of Congress Cataloging in Publication Data

Hilton, John Buxton.
   The Hobbema prospect.

   I. Title.
PR6058.I5H6   1984   823'.914   84-13335
ISBN 0-312-38828-4

First published in Great Britain by William Collins Sons & Co. Ltd.

First U.S. Edition

10 9 8 7 6 5 4 3 2 1

The Hobbema Prospect

CHAPTER 1

It was curious, Anne Cossey thought, why one remembered certain things so vividly, for no logical reason. There were incidents that stood out over the years: a critical moment of delirium in a childhood fever, a corner of conversation at an indifferent party. There was no reason for some things to stick, yet somehow she knew that today's homecoming would.

Today was understandably different. She had come home in the middle of the afternoon. Nobody had wanted to delay her, everyone had urged her to go. Kenworthy was out. One of the men had come back with a bottle of Jugoslav Riesling, and they had drunk it out of office cups. The journey home had been unpressed, a welcome change. She had sat back in a corner seat, seeing the streets, parks, back gardens and railway platforms of south-east London in an unusual ambiance.

She let herself into the deserted flat. It was shabby, worn, yet too many things were not far enough gone to compel replacement: an electric bar fire from the 1960s; LP sleeves—mostly *Nostalgia*. But it was a nostalgia that, once one had revived it, one did not want to revive a second time: early Spinners, Matt Monro, vintage Bee Gees. Her Athena blocks did nothing for the room any more—or for her: Brueghel's *Flemish Proverbs*, Seurat's *Grande Jatte*. She was going to leave them here. It seemed an unnecessary twist of the knife to bequeath to her mother two rectangles of discoloured (or rather undiscoloured) wallpaper. And God knows what horrors her mother would find to replace them with. There were signs that she was growing out of her belated psychedelic period.

Anne went into her bedroom, where most of her belong-

ings were packed into cardboard cartons begged from the
off-licence and supermarket. She changed out of her white
blouse and grey skirt, conscientiously compliant with the
office parameters as to sleeve-length, neckline and exposure
of calf. Not that anybody was ever fierce about the rules,
Kenworthy least of all. He never gave the impression that he
knew there was such a document as the Code, and ever since
Anne had worked there, there had been a gradual trend over
the edges. Twice in her time there had been Amendments,
mainly to legalize current practices. Some of the girls simply
pleased themselves, anyway, but Anne was by nature a
complier.

She looked in the mirror. Howard was not given to compli-
ments. He was by no means inarticulate, but verbal gymnas-
tics embarrassed him. Yet not so long ago he had told her
that her face had the perfect imbalance. He had read somewhere or other that if the left half of someone's face was in
exact equilibrium with the right, then that person's looks
could only be ordinary. It was the slight differences, perhaps
below the level of conscious perception, that made faces
interesting—and beautiful. She experimented now with a
sheet of paper, first over her face, then over the mirror, its
straight edge plumb down the middle of her nose. The result
was twofold and contradictory. At one angle, the two sides
seemed exact replicas of each other, condemning her to
eternal mediocrity. At another, there were such differences
that the two halves scarcely seemed to belong to the same
person. She was sure her nose was just a fraction too long and
too thin, her chin too soft-spirited, her chestnut hair too
banal, the ensemble too oval. But it did not matter, did it, as
long as Howard loved her that way—or said he did. Long
might he go on saying it! He had told her that her five feet
four inches were the ideal height for a woman, according to a
table he had seen in a magazine, that her age was precisely
the right few years younger than his. She blessed him for the
things he unearthed in magazines. They seemed to have been

written with her in mind.

The key grated in the latch. Her mother must have got off early, too. But—oh no!—two voices—and Radio Two switched on the moment they were in the room. Anne wished she were a mountaineer. She wanted to climb out of the window, do a hand-traverse to the fire-escape, betake herself from rooftop to rooftop, come gently to earth blocks and streets away. If only she could vanish! And the feeling was none the less strong for the knowledge that this was the last time she would be trapped like this. She was only going to be trapped for a matter of minutes—but trapped was trapped. She came out of her bedroom and greeted the two women with filial insincerity.

It was Angela again, taller than her mother, older than her by a few years, probably. It was hard to tell, because Angela was better at reducing her age than Jean Cossey was. And she obviously spent more on herself, had a more rewarding frame to work on. Angela was three inches taller than Anne, stood a full head higher than Anne's mother, which made one wonder how long it would be before Jean Cossey started looking like a little barrel. Jean Cossey's injudicious magenta two-piece did not cling to her; yet it drew immediate attention to her lifebelt. And she had recently had her hair done in a frizzy style that suited neither the shape of her head, nor the contours of her face, nor her place of work, nor her—

Anne's mother had known Angela all of ten days. Angela was the latest in a lifetime of raving friendships. Anne did not know where they had met: at some enforced sharing of a café-table, most likely. For two or three weeks it would be *Angela for Queen*, and then they would have a flaming row.

It was a pity it had to be Angela, just on the eve of her wedding. Angela seemed to find marriage somehow amusing, as if there were something archaic in having had an orthodox engagement, in being in love with one man, in going into it firmly believing that it was going to last.

'I'm just going down to Butcher's to see they know what's what for tomorrow.'

Anything to be out of the flat for the next half-hour. Angela looked at her, faintly laughing, faintly sneering: a woman who saw through everything, or thought she did, she had seen everything before and treated it all with scorn. Every detail in that flat at that moment etched itself into Anne's memory. She had, of course, no way of knowing that the trigger-factor would be murder.

CHAPTER 2

Outsiders were saying that Kenworthy was smouldering to fulmination point, but his staff saw no evidence of it. He treated them with a slightly archaic courtesy. There was a remote serenity about him: as if he had chosen serenity to help him weather out this phase.

Promoted to Chief Superintendent, he was whiling away his last few years in command of an indoor department. There were men, it was said, who wanted him inside—not poking about into some of the curious things that were going on at the Yard at this time. So they had him shunting paper about: dead files, stillborn casework, old master-plans that had foundered. Sometimes an investigating officer had known for certain, but there had been nothing safe to take before a jury. Sometimes there had been no hacking a way through the jungle. Now all these bits and pieces were going to be computerized. It was Kenworthy's job to decide what. Things were going to be brought together that had not come together before. Retrieval was going to be immediate. An argument oscillated. Was a man's brain an imperfect computer? Or was a computer an imperfect brain? Could a computer have flair? Unless you'd spent a lifetime rubbing shoulders with vital discrepancies, could you recognize them when you saw them? Kenworthy talked about trigger-factors until people hid their smiles. Every trigger-factor had to be cross-referenced. When Peter Griffiths dropped a bit of the wrapping of a wine-gum packet in the course of a break-in, that was a low-level trigger-factor. Griffiths liked the comfort of something flat and sweet clinging to his tongue while he worked.

At his left hand, Kenworthy had his feeders, civilians, screening files for him to read: there was enough of the stuff for a lifetime of man. On his right were the labourers at his keyboards, programming what he filtered out to them. He did not give a damn about their daisy-wheels, their interfaces and their floppy discs. He did not care what went on inside a silicon chip. But he would have liked something to happen that might give the job significance.

In the meanwhile, he acted patience, treating his staff with urbane respect. It was characteristic of him to attend the wedding of a girl he hardly knew, but whose charm and competence had struck him.

Anne had charm. She had poise, and she did not create the impression that anyone had taught her either of these. She did not dress differently from anyone else in the office, and yet she looked different. Anne Cossey was a natural.

CHAPTER 3

It was no way to start a honeymoon: air-controllers defecting in Spain, Gatwick milling, fat women with music-hall North Country voices monopolizing the concourse seats in their creased pink and powder blue Crimplene. The newly-wed Lawsons had to pay for a hotel bedroom that they hadn't budgeted for. The insurance would cough up—eventually. They had had to cash two of their travellers' cheques: corn in Egypt. And they had had to share a dinner table with a corpulent pair who had aggressively ignored them, conversing in some Central European gutturality.

Anne was determined not to be jaded, though jaded was what she knew she was. The last day was over that she would spend in her mother's flat, the last hours there unending. There was something, she knew, that her mother was on the verge of trying to say, but she could not articulate it. Anne had slipped away whenever she had looked as if she were about to make a start. And her mother had made this new friend, too. Heaven protect her from her mother's friendships! She would go without friends for months, then someone new would be filling her life. Why did her friendships always have to be so absorbing, so exhausting— and so often disastrous? God knew where her mother had picked this one up.

Howard would have preferred the registry office. Inside herself, Anne had wanted church. Getting married ought to be as spiritual as you could make it. But she had not pressed a case. She was scared of boring Howard with spirituality. But then her mother let loose something that she must have been bottling up for weeks, about something not coming up to her expectations. Did anything, ever? Anything but the altar-rail was tawdry, second-rate. When Anne's mother pleaded from the heart, she was a dab hand at putting her heart into it. Even after twenty years of constantly getting trapped by it, you could be worn down by her bleating sincerity. Anne gave way: stabs of conscience about the devil she'd been to her mother all these years. In all truth, their life as a one-parent family could have been worse. Her mother, not counting unpredictable tangents, had been something of a miracle-worker. So Anne had told Howard she had changed her mind, and he was too good-natured to be anything more than mildly exasperated. But this would be it, wouldn't it? They couldn't go on chopping and changing for ever.

She had become Mrs Howard Lawson at an altar-rail in a Pooterish South London High Street. Women had lined the pavement to watch her come out, in her white organdie, severely buttoned to her throat. If there was any criticism of her wedding-dress, it was that it was too austere. She and her mother had worked at it together, a task not beyond either of them, though the antagonism it had engendered was not to be believed. At the reception, the bar had swarmed with new in-laws. Beery detectives had edged together, talking internal politics: Howard was a detective-sergeant. And Shiner Wright, his inspector, had proposed the only toast of the day worth listening to.

'When a detective marries, it affects the whole Yard. I feel as if it's not only Howard who's married Anne. It's all of us.'

Laughter: and a smile from Kenworthy, who had brought a rather beautiful set of Bruges lace dressing-table runners. He had not stayed long, but it had been good—unexpected— of him to have come at all.

And there were girls from Anne's office there, some of them with weirdos in tow that she'd never have associated with them. Anne was civilian personnel on one of the Yard's collating teams, one of those on Kenworthy's left hand, though he could know her only as a name, a sharp intelligence, a working conscience—and power of recall for which people nowadays installed computers. Howard had come in one lunch-hour, needing info, and she had been the dog-watch that had helped him scrabble through tatty folders that had not been processed yet. That was how it had all started. And now one of Howard's stable-mates was waiting to rush them round London in a borrowed Jag. They found the airport jam-packed and no more flights to Spain today.

Anne felt near to nervous exhaustion. She hoped that at bedtime Howard would realize how all-in she was. It wasn't first-night nerves. They had had enough sex to have risen above clumsiness, to know they were compatible. Compatible? They could not exist without each other.

But tonight, in the chain-standardized, twin-bedded room, she did nothing to entice him. If he was bursting at the

seams, she'd try to say No without making him feel rejected.
But no—she knew she wouldn't. If it were like that, she'd let
him. But it ought to be special, the first time in their
permanent status. It had to establish them. She'd once seen a
paperback sex manners manual in his room. Maybe it had
had a paragraph, warning him of this very setback. And,
indeed, he asked quietly now, 'Worn out?'

'I'm sorry, Howard. Maybe we'll wake in the night.'

'I've brought my little travelling alarm.'

'Let's leave it to nature.'

She woke and he didn't. She woke from one of those
dreams that are so real that it is a relief to jerk out of them, to
reorientate oneself, disbelieving at first in the faint light of an
unfamiliar room. She remembered where she was and how
she came to be there. But she was still disturbed. It would not
help to try to go back to sleep. She knew from experience that
she would sink back into that dream.

It was an odd dream, terrifying, and yet without events.
Nothing happened in it. Nothing threatened to happen. She
was in a place, and the place frightened her. She was trapped
in the dream, yet she was looking into it from the outside. She
recognized the dream at once, always, a theatre of fright. Yet
she had no idea of its location. There were two rows of trees,
and they bordered a sandy roadway. It could have been
Hobbema's *Avenue*, but these were not the trees of the
Dutchman's painting. Unlike Hobbema's, they converged
on a house—which she never could properly picture when
she was awake. She had dreamed the dream since long before
she had ever visited a picture gallery, so it could not possibly
be Hobbema. And until she had started buying reproductions for herself, they had had very few pictures worth
looking at in the Cossey household.

The dream came irregularly. Sometimes the interval was
so long that she forgot she had ever dreamed it. Then, at the
beginning of her teens, she began to believe that it came as a
forecast of bad news: before she had had tonsillitis, and had

lost a part in a school play; before her mother had inexplic-
ably upped sticks and taken them away from Broadstairs,
where she was sublimely happy, to go and live in a dirty little
industrial town in the North-West. The dream always
seemed a signpost to the undesirable—and yet that was not
quite the truth. Sometimes she dreamed the dream and
waited for something wretched to happen, and nothing did.
So she would latch on to something trivial, some petty aggro,
convince herself that the prophecy had been fulfilled, that
she was safe again.

But why dream it on her wedding-night? Was it some part
of her inner self, uneasy about her decision? Was it a warning
about tomorrow's flight? Was something awful going to
happen in Spain?

She pushed such imbecilities away. Wasn't she adult—
now more adult than ever? She looked over at Howard, who
had lost the sheets from his shoulders and was sleeping
without vest and pyjama jacket. *With this body I thee worship.*
He would know how to kill this nightmare. But she did not
wake him. She was reluctant to talk to him about fantasies.
There was something fortifying about Howard, something
astringent about his materialism. He must not come to think
of her as a creature of rarefied fancies. She got up to pull the
sheets back over him, closed her eyes and tried to force the
trees to materialize, but now they would not. So now she
knew how to get rid of them. Challenge them to come back.
Simple.

In the morning, before they were out of bed, there was a
phone call from their travel agency. The Spaniards were still
on strike, so they would be flown to Portugal, taken on by
coach. Their flight was not till three this afternoon. She drew
the curtains: a steady rain was falling. The purpose-built-up
Surrey landscape was a grey vacuity. A jet was climbing
steeply into the murk. The day crept forward at a wretched
pace. There could be a better decor for a hung honeymoon
than Horley, Surrey. They had to avoid spending money.

Anne had not flown before and was moderately apprehensive of take-off. As they juddered up through heavy cloud, she was grateful for Howard's confident hand. Then somewhere over Biscay the atmosphere cleared. On the final approach to Faro she caught sight of a Noddy suburban train taking a curve. The world became golden-warm and palm-fringed. They were driven to the frontier and changed coaches there. By some sickening miracle, the women in creased Crimplene were still alive and making it towards the bingo at Torre-molinos. Dusk had taken a grip before they moved forward from Ayamonte. It was a nocturnal hell-ride to Malaga.

Not till the mid-small hours were they set down in their small resort, whose nucleus was still a fishing village. There was an unEnglish warmth in the air, a sweetness of un-English blossoms, a fragrance of citrus foliage. They carried their bags through a silent, cloistered plaza. The street-lamps accentuated the shadows of Moorish arcades, and unseen beyond the walls they could hear the sibilance of surf on shingle.

On their bedside tables, a supper of monastic simplicity was waiting on trays: bread, butter, cheese and mountain ham, carafes of red wine and a bottle of Lanjaron water. The night was mild. It would have been unthinkable not to have flung their balcony doors wide open. A beach stretched below them, a whisper of gentle breakers.

She slept for two hours, woke between five and six. The spreading red dawn silhouetted the shell of an ancient watch-tower. Men were hand-hauling a net up the beach, a ritual unchanged for centuries. Howard was sitting up reading, waiting for her.

She got up and went to him. There was little fondling, no talk. Afterwards, he filled their glasses with what was left of the wine.

'That was it, wasn't it?'

'The sum of all things.'

'I'll believe you this time, if you say you heard surf.'

Because when she closed her eyes in that kind of happiness, it was always surf she said she heard and saw, a silver filigree of surf. Howard had a contented way of smiling when she was being whimsical. It wasn't quite a smile of permissive disbelief, though he himself never talked capriciously. He always seemed gratefully surprised that a woman so different from himself should seem to want only him.

CHAPTER 4

Anne talked with lyrical abandon. She believed that when people slept, their souls went journeying. In this still largely unspoiled corner of Andalusia, she found plenty to rhapsodize about.

But a good deal of her talk was mundane, and she was uncomfortably aware of it. For a honeymoon, she was talking a good deal too much about her mother—yet she seemed unable to stop herself. Howard did not complain, but he sometimes sat with an arrested smile when she embarked on some 'new' anecdote. When he came to talk about it afterwards—when he came to have to talk about it, to Shiner Wright and the redoubtable Kenworthy—it showed through to those ruthless sizers-up that his patience had been beginning to wear thin.

They went to Granada, and because it was out of season, had the courts of the Alhambra largely to themselves. They sat in the life-giving sunshine in the Generalife Gardens and Anne compulsively told her husband again of their cruel migration from the Thanet coast to some hell-hole in the North when she was four and a half years old.

It had been irrational, chaotic to a child. Quite certainly there must have been a fairly simple explanation for it. But Anne's mother, even when Anne was grown up, had always refused to discuss it. Howard found Jean Cossey in many ways an estimable woman. Stand-up comics' mother-in-law jokes need have no part in his life. But there were things about her that defied understanding. Was she deep—or cheap? It was, of course, a question that he never asked aloud.

The upheaval had happened at the age when Anne's memory was just beginning to take a grasp on things. She and her mother had lived on the outskirts of Broadstairs, near to North Foreland, on the lip of the estuary, in a road that led down to a cliff-sheltered beach. She started school, at a private kindergarten a couple of avenues away. It was an old-fashioned, tone-conscious little academy. It had its own uniform, of which she was extravagantly proud: a pudding-basin hat with a velvet band, skirt, pullover, blazer and socks, all in sober navy with Cambridge blue trimmings. And at half past three every afternoon, when her mother met her laughing at the gate, they as often as not went straight for a picnic to an unfrequented little cove that they reached under a natural arch in the chalk. It was a long first term at school, a long late spring, a long early summer.

Then suddenly, without prologue, without preparation, came a morning when she learned that she was not going to school. Her uniform was not on her bedroom chair. In its place was an old outfit that she hated because she was not grown-up in it: a sun-bleached dress that she had had before she was old enough for school. It was now much too short for her.

'I know she had sold my uniform. She had advertised it on a card in the post-office window. Yet I don't know how I know that.'

They went by train, crossed London, and then in another train for many hours, to a place called Slodden-le-Woods, though where the woods were was a local joke. The power station had ogreish cooling towers. The water in the canal was black and smelled of oil and supported no kind of life at all. Early-morning workmen left oysters of phlegm on grey pavements. Anne hated Slodden: she could not even go to school there at first, because of some awkwardness about her birth-date. And there were complications because her mother had to go out to work—dirty, repetitive work, for which she left the house in a man's boiler-suit. She had to be in the factory by eight every morning, and Anne had to be dragged along the street in all weathers to the infant-minding Mrs Gregory, who was overweight and bad-tempered, and who laughed at Anne's precise turn of speech.

'I lost my identity. My mother made us start calling ourselves Carter. In Broadstairs, we had been Cresswells. It was only when we came to live in London that we became Cosseys. She never explained it to me. I just thought that when people moved to a different place, they were called by a different name. I thought it happened to everyone. Sometimes in Slodden I forgot I was no longer Anne Cresswell, and once or twice I actually came out with the wrong name. People looked queerly at me.'

There were some things that she did not tell Howard about her mother. Her thoughts about Stella Davidge, for example. It was an old file that she had handled, a similarity of circumstances that was frightening. Yet there were half a dozen good reasons why her mother, known for the last thirteen years as Jean Cossey, could not have been Stella Davidge. There were things about Jean Cossey that could never have belonged to Stella Davidge's background. Northwood Hills? Stockbroker's Metroland? Not Jean Cossey. Her mother did not even speak that kind of English. She still had more than a trace of North Country in her speech, though she did her best to hide it. Well, it was always possible that Stella Davidge's mother had had a Lancashire or Yorkshire connection. Even the landed gentry up there sometimes spoke with a noticeable accent.

They had laughed at Anne's speech at that school at Slodden. That school, when her birthday finally fitted into the system, did not have a uniform. It did not even have a proper playground, only a yard, in which boys scuffled, and where the fifty-a-side football game put any passing girl in peril. Anne could not even understand the language of that playground. The other children distrusted her with a hard rancour that went back deep into their tribal defences. Even when holidays came, there was no release. She had to go back to Mrs Gregory again: Mrs Gregory, who blew on her sandwich when it had fallen on the floor, and raged at her when she would not eat it.

They were in Slodden-le-Woods for three years. They did not come to London to live until Anne was nearly seven. There had never been any explanation of the episode. But some things about her mother had not been changed by their period of misery. Jean Cossey's work brought her home exhausted in the evenings, but she never shirked sharing the things that the child needed to have shared: *Magic Roundabout* or a chapter from *Pooh*. But there were some things that Anne learned never to ask about. Her paternity was one of them; the reason for Slodden was another.

'Financial crisis, obviously,' Howard had said, the first time he had heard all this.

'It was certainly that, but I always thought—I always knew—that there was more to it than that. If it was only money she was desperate for, she could always have gone to Egbert.'

'Who on earth was Egbert?'

'An uncle?' he almost added—but he was not given to that type of jibe.

'Oh, Egbert wasn't a person. It was her pet name for some money that she had, some savings that she was looking after for me. I think she might have got the name from the idea of a nest-egg. And I never had any idea how she had been able to save up Egbert. In those days, it didn't occur to me to wonder. I suppose I used to think that all families had their Egberts.'

'Most Egberts don't last all that long.'

'That's the amazing thing—one of the reasons I'm grateful to her. Egbert did last. I remember once being furious with her because she wouldn't let Egbert buy me an ice-cream. My Broadstairs uniform came out of Egbert. So did my trip to France in the fifth form at school. And our wedding reception. And the balance left over was our wedding-present cheque.'

'Good old Egbert!'

'It was something she kept quite separate from the house-keeping. The job she had at Slodden was terrible. Our standard of living wasn't much above survival, after she had paid Mrs Gregory. I can see that now. But Egbert was still intact when we came back down south.'

'Maybe Egbert's solvency varied.'

'I don't think the trouble had just to do with money. I always thought it had to do with Mr Camel-Leopard.'

'Egbert's brother-in-law?'

'Mr Camel-Leopard was just my name for him. The word camelopard was in one of my picture-books. I thought Mr Camel-Leopard looked like one. You know what I mean?'

'Roughly.'

'He was waiting higher up the road one afternoon when my mother met me out of school in Broadstairs. He was a fairly good-looking man, I suppose, quite old. Nowadays, I'd probably think quite young. I thought he looked sinister, but that may just have rubbed off on me from what happened afterwards. I could see my mother was upset to see him. She dragged me down the road faster than I could walk, and she would not let us go to our special beach. I remember throwing a tantrum. I can see now, though, why she would not let us go there. He could have trapped us down there, if the tide had come in. Instead, she made us walk all the way along the clifftop to Cliftonville. As compensation, she took me to an Italian place opposite Margate Harbour, and she bought me an ice-cream with two sparklers alight in it. We went home by bus.'

'I never cease to wonder at how much you remember.'

'Probably that's because I've thought about it so often since. We threw Mr Camel-Leopard off, but there was nothing very clever about that. He could have followed us to Margate, if he'd wanted to. But he didn't have to. He came round that evening. I knew who he was, although I was in bed, and my window was at the back, overlooking cornfields and the sea.'

'You knew?'

Howard was poking fun in the nicest possible way.

'One of those things—not all that hard to explain. I had him very much on my mind, and unless it was a neighbour wanting to borrow something, we didn't often have evening visitors. I could hear voices downstairs, though not what they were saying. I know they were angry with each other. And I don't know how long after that that we made our move to Slodden. But you can't fool children. I knew there was a connection.'

'You have a wonderful way of knowing things. You'd do well in my job.'

'Well—didn't you solve your best case yet because of something I dug out for you in our office? I say—do let's go and see the Gypsies.'

There were cliff-dwellers on the Sacromonte side of the city who were said to put on a less inhibited brand of flamenco than one saw in the cafés. The guide-book said steer clear of them, but Anne and Howard were their own travellers.

One afternoon towards the end of their honeymoon, they had tired of beach routines and had taken a local bus up into the Sierra to a dazzling white village. A man in the street with a falcon on his wrist was a casual ingredient of the scene: no one paid any attention to him. They walked down a track such as Don Quixote might have ridden.

In this setting Anne chose to return to the subject of her identity. She had never known more than the name and occupation of her father: Peter Burne Pennyman, Shipping Clerk. But the lack of that knowledge had never soured her life. No one had ever embarrassed her over it. It had been no bar to her employment on confidential work in a public department. Howard had fallen in love with her not caring a whit about the seam in her background. True, she had been anxious when it had come to meeting his parents. Howard's father was something in banking—something that ranked above High Street manager, tucked away in the City square mile. His mother was the sort of woman whose coffee mornings were never casual. The couple must have had their reservations about Anne. Even at the reception, Anne had felt that they had not lost all trace of them. But they were disciplined people who, once they had decided to repress their anxieties, would never willingly let them seep out

'It's funny, you know, Howard. Pennyman was a name my mother never wanted me to know.'

They had been watching a field labourer attending to irrigation channels, a complex system of ditches that got the mountain water to every individual furrow in a field of heavenly carnations.

'It was the Moors who taught the Spaniards to do that,' Howard said. 'The hidalgos thought it beneath their dignity to work on the land.'

'Pennyman—she did not even want me to see my birth certificate. When I needed it, she said she couldn't find it. I had to have it for my passport. I thought it was going to stop me from going on that school trip to France. The deposit had already been paid—by Egbert.'

'Understandable. Something she wasn't all that proud of. We've nothing to gain from trying to dig it all up. Why bother with things that make no odds in our life? Whoever your Mr Pennyman was, I'm grateful to him. I wouldn't want your genes and what-do-you-call-ems any different from what they are.'

Then a new thought crossed her mind. Had there been a Pennyman in Stella Davidge's background? There must be skeletons in cupboards, even in Metro-Tudorland. But Howard was now kissing her shoulder. The man crouching over his muddy gutters did not look up. They commanded a massive sweep of coast from Torre del Mar to Los Berenguelas. They climbed down the bed of a dried-out arroyo. But still her mind dwelled on Pennyman.

Her mother had seemed startled when she came home from school demanding her birth certificate for the passport application. Anne had never seen the document. She only knew in theory that such things existed. At the age of sixteen, she had never had to ask for it before.

'I'm trying to remember where I put it,' her mother said. But she would not go through her papers in Anne's presence. For two or three days Anne nagged her.

'It must have gone astray when we went up north.'

'What am I going to do? I shan't be able to go.'

At sixteen, alternatives have a habit of looking like extremes.

'Don't be silly. There are ways and means.'

'Hadn't you better write to Somerset House or something?'

Her mother said she would go herself to get the certificate. She spent a day on her own in central London. But she came back empty-handed.

'They are sending it by post.' But it did not come.

'Civil servants!'

She was away again all day, and this time when she returned in the early evening, she did have the document. Anne held out her hand for it, but her mother was reluctant to pass it over. Things were not easy between them at this period. They were always misunderstanding each other, as if deliberately. There had been almighty rows over lesser incidents than this. Jean Cossey dropped the buff envelope on the table and left the room.

Anne shouted through to the kitchen: 'Who was Peter Burne Pennyman, Shipping Clerk? And why isn't my name Pennyman?'

'Isn't Cossey good enough for you? You can forget about him. Put him right out of your head. He never troubled himself over us.'

'How come I was born in Carshalton?'

'I happened to be living there at the time, and I rather wanted to have you with me.'

'Ha-ha. Mum's made a funny.'

'I've often wondered,' Mrs Howard Lawson said to her husband on the winding road below Frigiliana, 'whether Mr Pennyman was Mr Camel-Leopard.'

'In either case, it's a pity he didn't think of deed-poll.'

'I mean—were we hiding from my own father in Broadstairs?'

'Does it matter all that much?'

Was there something in his tone that told of wearying tenderness? For once she had the sense to start talking about something else. It was their last whole day in the Mediterranean landscape. When would they be able to afford to see Spain again? Tonight they were going to celebrate. They had a small kitty of pesetas unspent, would be able to drink a more distinguished Rioja than usual with their candlelit dinner.

A telegram was waiting for them on the board. They assumed that it was from their tour operator, giving them their homeward instructions: the air traffic people had now changed their tactics to one-day stoppages.

But Howard, after reading the message, turned away when Anne held out her hand for it. He took it over to the window and read it again, as if he were unsure of its meaning. It had been written out in longhand by a clerk to whom the copying of a foreign tongue was a laborious business.

Howard folded the telegram and put it away in his pocket. Anne looked at him inquiringly, but it was not until they were back in the bedroom with the balcony that he began to prepare her for shock.

'Darling—'

Anne's mother had died. There was a lack of further information that left them utterly helpless. Anne did not disbelieve the news—she could not disbelieve it—but it did not seem real to her—yet.

And at first impact, neither of them saw anything ominous in the fact that the telegram had been signed *Wright*.

CHAPTER 5

The journey home was messy, hot, crowded and delayed. Howard found Anne's composure surprising. She had little to say, and the nearest she came to pathos was with her naive, 'I wish it wasn't true.'

'I'm afraid that it is true, darling.'

She looked away out of the streaked window of the aircraft. They were flying at thirty-odd thousand feet and the cloud formation below them was punctuated by pinnacles of white fluff. At Gatwick they looked around for a message, but no one was paging them. Howard went to make a phone call. When he came back he was looking even more solemn than before.

Duty had brought Howard Lawson into the presence of death: street accidents in his uniform days; an overdose suicide; two murders since he had been in Shiner's squad. But they had been the type of murder more common in fact than in fiction. Drearily domestic, they had posed no problems. He had seen blood, human organs drastically exposed. He had seen strangers' tears. But he had never been personally involved.

He had been taught theory, elements of applied psychology, including some notes on the transference of guilt, by a sergeant-instructor hard-boiled by a lifetime of other people's miseries. This man had impressed Howard: he was not the one to talk about non-material values unless he believed what he was saying. Death came as a shock—so people clutched at things to blame themselves for. And when they had lived close to the dead, they did not usually have to look far to find something to plague their haunted consciences with.

Anne was going to suffer. Her relations with her mother had been equivocal. She was not going to be short of grounds for self-torture. Howard had learned enough about her in Spain to believe that she was going to be difficult to handle. Because not only, Shiner had told him over the phone, had Jean Cossey's death been suicide, it had been suicide in a loathsomely stage-managed manner. And it had been backed up by a letter to the coroner that could not have been better guaranteed to break Anne's heart if it had been written with that intent.

Jean Cossey had first blunted cowardice with gin. The seal from the bottle-top was duly found in her kitchen. She had taken it into her bathroom, where in her final convulsion the unstoppered bottle had been knocked into the bath. Analysis of the bath-water suggested that she had drunk at least four-fifths of that bottle. The pathologist believed she must have been near to alcoholic poisoning. Jean Cossey had electrocuted herself. She had done so on the principle of the electric chair, with a simple but effective extension from a live lead to foil that she had taped to her head and to a wire bracelet round her left wrist. The neutral lead had been connected to one ankle, under water. The terminals had been connected to a length of new cable which had been cobbled into the oven element of her cooker, two rooms away. The timer had been set to switch itself on at ten-thirty in the evening.

Detective-Inspector Wright had been trained by Kenworthy and had an eye for detail. His Detective-Sergeant Izzard—normally the task would probably have fallen to Howard—had found a crumpled supermarket till receipt in the bottom of Mrs Cossey's shopping-bag: for one item—the price of the gin. In her pedal-bin was the bag in which she must have brought home the cable from a multiple hardware store round the corner. In the bottom of that bag was another receipt—undoubtedly for the cable.

The note to the coroner was short, shallowly derivative, childishly naive:

Dear Sir,

I am sorry for the trouble I am causing. When you have given the whole of your life for something you no longer have, there is nothing left.

It is all too empty now, without what I have always lived for.

Yours truly,
Jean Cossey

It had been written with a cheap and rather blotchy ballpoint, which was found among a miscellany of its kind in a jar on a kitchen shelf. The notepaper and envelope matched a pad and packet in a drawer of the cabinet. Shiner Wright got succinct papers together for the coroner and sent Sergeant Izzard off on another case. Howard treated Anne with great delicacy.

They needed her at the mortuary for identification, and she faced up to that with an aplomb that surprised him. Afterwards he took her to a quiet restaurant and told her more than he had originally intended about the details of her mother's death. And again her reaction was not what he would have expected. She was pale, and she did not speak at once when he had come to the end. He was not sure that it had all sunk in. But she remained in control of herself. Maybe the full reaction was going to be delayed—perhaps even for a day or two.

'I find it very difficult to believe,' she said at last, firmly but calmly.

'I'm sure you do.'

'Nothing could be less like her character.'

'We can never know what's going on in someone else's mind,' he said.

'You didn't know her, Howard. The sort of life we led, we knew each other inside out. I'm sure that's why there were times when we didn't get on. We knew each other too well, we got sick of each other. Oh, she was volatile: she had her ups and downs. She had her sentimental moments. She could listen to *Stars on Sunday*—weepy hymns—and she'd weep. Now and then. A sort of indulgence. But that was one off. When she was up against it, she was the hardest-headed woman I've ever known. She had to be, to have managed our lives the way she did. I mean, I never knew why we went to Slodden. Slodden was the dregs—but she saw to it that we never sank quite to the bottom. She was an optimist, Howard. If she hadn't seen silver linings where there were none, we could not have survived. And the wording of that silly note is not hers. She would never for a moment have contemplated taking her own life because I had left home to get married. That is perfectly absurd.'

'The human mind is a funny thing, Anne. I'm afraid we are up against something that words can't fight—the facts of the matter.'

'That's just what I can't accept, Howard—the so-called facts. She knew nothing about electricity. She couldn't have changed a fuse. She hated putting a new bulb in, in case it lit up while it was still in her hand. If she tried to fit a plug on to something she'd bought—a hair-drier, a toaster—I always looked to see whether she'd fixed the brown lead to the earth-pin. All she knew about electricity, she said, was that it could bite: and she left it alone. Besides, there was a lot that she was looking forward to. There was this new friend she'd found. I didn't like her, but they were getting on famously.

She wasn't too old to make something of her new freedom. She said to me so often, these last few months, that she was looking forward to her fling.'

'You've been no brake on her freedom—especially since you've had a job.'

'Freedom from responsibility, freedom from set habits: don't you see that? Freedom from somebody else's timetable. She was a woman with a tremendous capacity for enjoying herself—but she had always put her responsibility to me first. That's the habit that it wasn't easy to break.'

'What about men friends—actively—recently?'

'Off and on. I've told you before—she often showed the most appalling judgement of people. She always thought they were what she would like them to be. Even at the age of seven, I tried to warn her off some of the men she made friends with. Not that they amounted to a procession, you understand. Just now and then.'

A difficult angle. Howard Lawson had formed his own impression of Jean Cossey's taste in men. He did not want to go too deeply into that just now.

'Maybe she had been let down by someone.'

'I can't think who it could be. And in any case, that wouldn't be a situation she hadn't handled before. More than once. She might be depressed about it—well, not so much depressed as angry. But she'd bounce back. She always did. She'd swear there'd never be another. And for three or four months—or weeks—or days—perhaps there wouldn't be. How soon are we going to be allowed into the flat?'

'I'll have to ask. I expect all the scene of crime stuff will be finished. And they've said publicly that they don't suspect foul play.'

'I want to go there. I want to go there now.'

Howard still had much to learn about his wife.

'We shan't be able to shift any of your stuff tonight,' he said.

'I don't want to shift any stuff. There's something I want to look at.'

'Something that can't wait?'

'I shan't sleep if I don't.'

He phoned Shiner's office and got clearance. It meant a taxi, and running the gauntlet of the neighbours' curiosity. And yet no one seemed to have been curious on the night Jean Cossey had died: there was no one who would admit to having heard or seen anything or anyone. Everything bore the lifeless look of quarters deprived of a woman's care. There was still a mug on the draining-board, decorated with the Colman's Mustard logo. Jean Cossey's gadgets were where she always kept them, too many for her racks and jars: whisks, spatulas, kitchen scissors jam-packed at drunken angles. The door of the oven was slightly ajar and there were scraps of oven dirt on the tiles in front of it: a legacy no doubt from the suicidal connection.

In the living-room there was a special kind of emptiness: cheap reproductions—Toulouse-Lautrec and Monet's poppies—pictures that would never give pleasure again; Jean Cossey's LP's—James Last, pop Galway, Abba. She had not listened to most of them for years, and Anne was never going to listen to them again. There was a *Woman's Own* and a shelf of paperbacks: Robbins, Hailey, Delderfield, Edwin Booth. The Booth was years old: *Four Marys*. Anne remembered how she had picked it out once when she was thinning their shelves for a jumble sale. And her mother had angrily snatched it back, as if she attached some sentimental value to it. And what added to the sense of pathos was the obvious evidence that all this had been gone over by the investigators, by Shiner and his team. Some things had not been put back exactly where they belonged. The snowstorm paper-weight that Anne had bought in the Eiffel Tower had changed places with a carved Bambi. The magazines by the skirting-board were in reverse order, the older ones now on top: *Family Circle* and a *Private Eye*: who could have brought that home?

Howard went straight into the bathroom, hunting down any relic of the gruesome that he felt ought to be concealed. In here the search had clearly had to be more fundamental. Talc had been spilled. Some of the all-but-empty phials from the medicine cabinet had been left out: soluble aspirin, vitamin capsules, a few dregs left over from a bronchial winter.

Anne went into her mother's bedroom, not pausing to take stock, but heading straight for the old walnut wardrobe. She opened it and plunged through the summer dresses, the cleaners' plastic covers. She reached down into the farthest corner.

'Howard—come here.'

She had brought out two bottles of Californian table wine, a jar of cocktail cherries, three-quarters full, a half-finished Haig Dimple and a Tia Maria.

'My mother wasn't what I'd call a drinking woman. I've known her go weeks, even months, without taking a drop. Then once in a while she'd have what she called a ball—usually in the first flush of misery after someone had stood her up. It never did her any good. She might get a bit flushed and giggly after the first couple of gins—but after another you'd soon see her nodding off to sleep. That was the only useful effect alcohol ever had on my mother. But she did like to think there was drink in the house. She didn't like to be caught out if anyone called. If someone gave her a bottle as a present—I remember, she won one not long ago in a raffle—it generally went straight into the wardrobe. She used to say that was two-thirds of the way out of temptation. Including this—and this—'

One was a bottle of Gordon's, the other a *Beefeater*, both with their seals unbroken.

'So why a receipt from a supermarket off-licence? Now I'm going to show you something else.'

She went to a free-standing broom-cupboard, and was for

a moment held up by the clutter. The moment she opened the door, everything fell out.

'What about this?'

She was holding a hank of years-old electric extension cable, its cotton covering badly frayed over both plugs.

'The man who wired this house didn't give much thought to where he was putting the power points. This is what my mother had to use when she wanted to iron and watch the telly at the same time. Howard, I want you to see whether it would reach from the cooker to the bath.'

He had already measured the distance with his eye, and he knew that it would. He said as much.

'No. Let's make sure.'

There were at least thirty feet of the cable, and it crossed the space easily.

'Howard, my mother wasn't mean. But she'd never spend money where she didn't have to. She wouldn't buy cable to kill herself while she had this on the premises.'

Howard's eyes had been travelling the room. He saw that Mrs Cossey's *Moo-Moo Dairies* calendar had been heavily ringed for a Tuesday still a week ahead.

'Of course, it's abundantly clear that she wasn't herself,' he said.

'You mean she was out of her mind? I don't believe that.'

'Anyone capable of killing herself must have been disturbed.'

'Not so disturbed as to buy gin when she'd two bottles in the house.'

'How can we be sure? We're talking about regions where even the experts won't commit themselves. I don't want to harp on this, darling, but I did speak on the phone to one of the first officers to come in here. He told me what he found.'

'He found my mother dead. That's a fact. My mother killing herself—that's an appearance. And it's ludicrous to think that she'd do it in this lunatic fly-trap manner. That note she wrote—is supposed to have written—when can I see it?'

'Tomorrow, for certain—at the inquest.'

'She'd never have written what you told me.'

'I can't guarantee that I gave you the precise words.'

'I must check her handwriting.'

'They'll have done that. Routine. They'll have found a sample somewhere.'

'I want you to tell Mr Wright about the gin and the cable.'

'I will.'

'Tonight. Now.'

'He'll be at home.'

'Then ring him at home.'

But that needed thought: ringing the DI at home about an open-and-shut case—Howard did not doubt that it was open and shut. The evidence wouldn't have been treated superficially: the seal from the bottle, the cable, the bag it was brought home in—

'Are you going to ring him—or shall I? I thought that in your line of business, time was supposed to be vital.'

She made for the phone. He reached it first and put a hand over hers.

'We don't want to stir up mares' nests.'

'Howard—there were strange things in my mother's life.'

Mr Camel-Leopard? Egbert?

'I haven't told you everything about her,' Anne said. 'There were strange things in her life before she had me.'

Mr Pennyman?

'Aren't you supposed to use your imagination, Howard? Suppose she didn't do this. Suppose someone else did it—set it up—isn't that the phrase you use? Wouldn't it be easy to plant check-out receipts and the rest?'

Howard took his hand off his wife's and started to dial. A minute and a half later, he put the phone back on its rest.

'He's coming round now.'

CHAPTER 6

After the first flurry of activity, the melancholy inertia of the
flat took over. Deprived of their owner, the trivial things that
had belonged to Jean Cossey seemed themselves defunct: the
bus ticket bookmark in the Catherine Cookson that she
would never finish; an Agatha Christie. Her reading had
been undemanding, for preference sentimental. But she
had read good things in her time. When Anne had been
growing up, she was always nagging her to read *Lord of the
Flies* and *Barchester Towers*—thereby creating consumer
resistance.

   She had often wondered just how intelligent her mother
really was. When Anne had tried to nail down her schooling,
she had always evaded the issue. But although she always
successfully dodged revealing the details, there were sequins
of pride that glistened. She had been to a High School. She
had passed the eleven-plus—which she always called winning a scholarship. She had lived for the library at school.
Maybe the books she had been guided through in class were
the only ones she truly appreciated. She had repeated time
and again that Eng. Lit. (*sic*) was the only school subject that
she had truly enjoyed.

   Howard was now sitting, tired, in the chair that had
always been her mother's. He lit a cigarette. He smoked too
many, but Anne had not said much about that—as yet. She
could not remain seated. There was an inner call to be up and
doing, but when she was on her feet there was nothing to do.
She went and shut herself in her old bedroom, a setting that
had played a large part in her adolescence. She had already
done most of her packing before the wedding, but some
things were still lying about—the juvenilia from her book-
shelves, her badminton racquet, a teddy-bear. It came as a

minor shock to her that the police had been through her things too. Her roll of posters had been interfered with. She had a map of the Paris Metro, a head and shoulders of Elton John.

Inspector Wright was a long time in coming: he had a sizeable quadrant of London to cross. When he did arrive, he was apologetic yet businesslike. Neither she nor Howard had known him at the time when he was making a name for himself as Kenworthy's winger. Howard knew him only as taskmaster—and, in general, a friendly spirit. He was a bit of a self-conscious oracle, phenomenally hard-working. It was obviously one of his things to be visibly ahead of his squad when it came to techniques, cross-references—and memory. Their working programme often seemed like a kind of competition. He usually won.

'I'm sorry to keep you up so late, Anne. You've had a terrible shock and a tiring journey, I know. But I take it you'll not be turning in to work in the morning.'

As a matter of fact, she had thought of doing so. She thought she ought to keep herself occupied. And there was still an unprocessed file she badly wanted to see again: Stella Davidge.

'It's up to you. But you'll be wanted at the inquest in the afternoon. And I'll have a word with Simon Kenworthy.'

Wright was supposed to be one of the best welfare officers in the Met. He looked after his team and their families.

'Now I believe you have something to tell me—to show me?'

Howard made as if to do the telling for her, but Wright held him off. She told him about the cable and the drinks cupboard. Wright nodded. It was not clear whether that was to acknowledge understanding, or because he was not at all surprised by this complication.

'So you are suggesting that somebody killed your mother?'

She sought words.

'If she didn't do it herself,' Wright said, 'that's the only alternative, isn't it? Do you know of anyone who was likely to?'

'Certainly not among her present acquaintances.'

'You seem to have a special way of saying that. Among present acquaintances—what of the past?'

Anne looked sideways at Howard. He must be dreading the Pennyman/Camel-Leopard scenario. She had to tell it all, but decided to keep it brief, to keep her terms adult. Then, without the childish labels, it all seemed stilted, unreal—and terribly intricate. Before she had finished, Wright had gone to his briefcase and brought out a document wallet. When she had done he waited a second, as if he thought there might be more to come.

'Your mother kept an address book. I expect you've seen this before.'

'I've seen her use it. It's a very old one. It was made clear to me, even in early childhood, that it was not for my eyes.'

'Some spirited children would have risen to that challenge,' Wright said, not without a twinkle. 'Didn't you sometimes want to check up on her, as you grew older?'

'Check up on her?'

'Men do predominate in that notebook.'

'A lot of the names there are dentists, plumbers, chimney-sweeps.'

'I dare say all of them were something,' Wright said. 'But some were strictly social, surely?'

'Obviously,' she said, after a pause.

'Is there anything else you think you ought to tell me about her?'

She was tempted to sidle from the issue, tempted even to resent it. But she took a grip on temptation.

'I can understand what you must be thinking, Mr Wright. My mother liked men's company. She needed the company of a nice man. Sometimes she assumed that a man was nice when he wasn't.'

'Which ones weren't?'

'I don't think I can really answer that. She didn't tell me everything. She kept remembering that she ought to set me an example. I think that thought always won the day—ultimately.'

'Always, Anne?'

Anne thought back. Nearly always. But in retrospect, even the exceptions had been harmless. There had been some poor specimens, but they had disappeared quickly from her mother's life. It seemed pointless to complicate Inspector Wright's vision at this stage with things about which she was basically unsure. And what about the woman she'd befriended a week or two before the wedding, that Angela? The only thing Anne really knew about her was that she didn't like her. Was she worth mentioning? Wright spoke again before she could.

'It may come to the point, Anne, where I shall want to go through this little notebook with you—if only to eliminate the chimney-sweeps. But we can't do that tonight. Let's just look at a few. The very last on the list, for instance.'

She had, of course, sneaked a look in her time, but not recently.

'Inkie Ingham. A Streatham telephone number. Ring any bells?'

'None whatever.'

'James Rafferty, Dulwich Village?'

'Domestic heating consultant.'

Wright flicked back a number of pages.

'One or two are so heavily scored out, you'd think she'd done it in a fit of bad temper. We may have to go to Forensic to take out the overlay. Stephen Matthewson, Blackpool?'

'I remember him. That's years ago.'

Just before they came to London. She was seven. Her mother could not have seen Stephen Matthewson more than three or four times.

'Don't trust my judgement of him,' she said. 'He seemed

decent enough at the time. I think I even had high hopes for him. But it fizzled out.'

'And Richard Foulkes, Accrington?'

'A pain in the neck. At least, that's what my mother said.'

Howard was wearing his non-blinking face, not looking at Wright—nor at her.

'I don't think those names are going to get us far, Mr Wright. I was still at a Lancashire primary school in those days.'

'So if you had remembered them, that would have been because they were memorable. Let's roll the years on a bit. Eric Talbot, Thornton Heath. Your judgement was better developed by that time.'

'It was. I was seventeen. I told her he was no good. We had the father and mother of a row.'

'Who won?'

'I never saw him again. My mother treated me for a week as if I'd personally deprived her.'

That phase of their lives had been bad.

Wright closed the book with a snap of finality.

'Would you have said that your mother was financially comfortable?'

'Sometimes far from it. Recently she's been getting by.'

'She had worked all her life?'

'She never did in our Broadstairs days. When we went to Lancashire, she had a revolting job on an assembly line. In London she worked in various places—shops, cafés, offices. For the last six or seven years she was receptionist at a driving school. She seemed to enjoy that.'

Wright produced two pass-books from a folder.

'She had two building society accounts. They are interesting. You may know about them already.'

'I don't know the details. I dare say they will not surprise me.'

'What pattern would you expect, then?'

'Difficult to say. I didn't even know there were two accounts.'

'Both opened on the same day,' he said. 'In nineteen-sixty-one. One for three thousand. One for two thousand. The one for two thousand went down fairly rapidly.'

'I can imagine.'

'Large monthly withdrawals in nineteen-sixty-two and nineteen-sixty-three. Nothing put back.'

'That would be what she—we—were living on.'

'There was a final big withdrawal—one thousand—in nineteen-sixty-three.'

'That would be when we went to Slodden.'

'Was Slodden such a spending spree?'

'As I remember it, quite the opposite.'

'The other account lasted very much longer.'

Egbert . . .

'There was a first withdrawal in nineteen-sixty-three.'

School fees and uniform—

'Then very little else—ten or twenty pounds at Christmas time—until nineteen-seventy-five. A hundred and fifty—'

Paris. Her fare. New clothes. Pocket money. It was a rat race against the other girls. That had mattered very much to her mother.

'A withdrawal to close the account a few days before your wedding. She could, of course, have made the paid-up shares over to you.'

'She said there were to be no strings—not even hints or suggestions. It was to be my money.'

For the first time, she knew, there was a crack in her voice.

'I owe my mother a great deal,' she said. 'She had guts, and she was loyal. Yet sometimes I think I know next to nothing about her. I do know she didn't kill herself.'

Wright did not commit himself. He waited to see whether her moment of emotion would produce anything else. When she withdrew into herself, he brought something else from his sheaf of documents. He handed her two birth certificates.

'I'd like you to look at these closely. Take your time. Tell me if there's anything that strikes you about them.'

COSSEY, Agnes Jean. 18th September, 1941. Farnworth General Hospital, Lancashire. Father: James Cossey. Mother: Mabel Anne Cossey, maiden name Dowe. Father's occupation: plasterer, of 18, Barrow Brow, Stonehill, Lancashire. Informant: James Cossey. Date registered: 26th September, 1941. P.R. Canfield, Deputy.

COSSEY, Anne. 4th July, 1959. General Hospital, Carshalton, Surrey. Father: Peter Burne Pennyman. Mother: Agnes Jean Cossey. Father's occupation: Shipping Clerk, of 4A Brook Buildings, Southampton. Informant: Agnes Jean Cossey, c/o Walwyn, Knutsford House, Carshalton. Date registered: 23rd July, 1959. J.W. Smith, Deputy.

'The same ink,' Anne said, when at last she looked up.
'That's not important. They use the same ink throughout the Registrar-General's Department: a composition that does not fade easily. But actually these documents were not written in Registrar-General's ink—only a chemical approximation to it. We have already established that. Anything else?'
She could not see what else he might be getting at.
'Look at the serial numbers. They are consecutive. And since these are supposed to be originals, separated in time by eighteen years and in space by two hundred miles, how can they have been written on forms that were neighbours in the book? They can only have come from a book unlawfully possessed. In fact, these are both forgeries.'
'They can't possibly be originals. Surely they're certified copies? I remember my mother going to London for them. She said she might as well get a copy of her own while she was about it.'
'They purport to be originals.'

She told him frankly about the episode of her passport.

'Thank you. And my apologies again for the hour. I had to press on with this, to tidy up my report to the coroner. Well—let's not call it tidy up. Let's say rewrite. If we could have got a clear verdict, well and good. A case out of the way, and law-abiding people could have got on with their lives. As it is—'

'As it is—?'

'Unanswered questions. No one on the landings, no one on the stairs heard or saw a thing. We shall have to ask them all again—shan't we, Howard?—a little more forcefully, perhaps. And ask the coroner for an adjournment.'

CHAPTER 7

It was a time for great kindness, for soft words, for tactfully steered conversations, a time when people's intentions were sometimes finer than their understanding. Anne needed to think, but when she managed to get time to herself, her own lack of understanding puzzled and frightened her. Would she ever understand anything again?

Wright had tactfully hinted that a month's adjournment would give him time to follow up complexities. The coroner, asserting his right to be in control, had quietly insisted on twenty-one days.

Howard's parents had been kind. Anne had been dreading their brand of kindness, expecting it to be self-conscious, excogitated—and off-beam. But this was not the way it worked out. Howard's father had the good sense to carry on with his own thing—his newspapers, the abstracts he brought home from his office. Howard's mother, with smooth self-discipline, stayed away from Anne's private affairs. Perhaps she felt that that was territory which any good woman and true would be prudent to steer clear of.

Anne knew what she feared, and she saw those fears materializing close under every surface.

Howard was kind. But he, of all people the one from whom she surely had the right to expect intuitive comprehension, was in fact the most bewildered. It hurt him, she could see, when his kindnesses did not evoke demonstrative responses. Perhaps he felt that his position as the rightful centre of her existence was being usurped. She tried to act up to his expectations—but knew she was acting.

Kindest of all was Kenworthy. For one reason or another, she did not actually go back to the office for two more working days, and then the weekend supervened. The funeral was on the Monday, so it was the Tuesday morning before she reported back for duty. The files on which she had been working the day before her wedding were still waiting for her, untouched in her absence. It was long-term material that she was passing up to Kenworthy after she had sifted it according to the principles he had laid down. She had just arranged her day's work in order of handling, when Kenworthy sent down for her. She was preceded into his office by a tray bearing coffee and biscuits for two.

She could not say that she knew Kenworthy well. Still less would she have believed that he knew very much about her. They had a working relationship. He had concisely let her know the form and content of what he wanted from her, and unlike some of her fellow toilers, she generally managed to give it to him. Kenworthy was a man of whom she always felt more than just slightly afraid. Even his serene courtesy was something to be afraid of. He was the spirit that parted the waters of their department. She could not conceive how anyone could give him less than their best.

He received her with avuncular familiarity. Within the next few minutes she was surprised by how much Shiner Wright must have talked to him about her. This was apparent not only from the detail he revealed, but from his whole attitude. Of all the people who had asked her questions in the last few days, he was the only one who seemed to have every fact at his fingertips. He knew what everything was about—and he sympathized unreservedly with her. She did not know that his reputation had been built up on precisely that ability to establish confidence; or that such confidence could be totally unfounded, if that was what suited his book.

He did not come straight at the matter. He had been to Spain, and had driven along the road from Malaga to Almunecar. He believed, though he was not sure, that he and his wife had lunched at the Lawsons' hotel.

'So you came back to disaster.'

'Unmitigated.'

'And one of the trigger-factors in this instance would appear to be birth certificates?'

'It seems so.'

How could she herself be untainted by the constructive dishonesty of those forgeries?

'Anne—how often have you come across false documentation in the dead files you've been handling here?'

Passports, now and then, even academic diplomas. But birth certificates? Not specifically. She recognized that she probably wouldn't. Once such a forgery was done, the perpetrator had a very strong chance of getting away with it. She said so.

'And to plunge into the heap, looking just for birth certificates, would be a daunting job? It almost makes me believe in computers,' he said.

They just hadn't the manpower to comb intensively through unindexed archives covering a quarter of a century. She said that, too.

'When you went to Paris, your mother went personally to get certified copies, and came back with originals. That was achieving the impossible. So we'll have to pay visits to some of our more illustrious forgers, won't we? That'll put wind up a few of them. You had a young mother, Anne.'

Do mothers ever seem young to their infants? She knew what Kenworthy meant. It was something she had always taken for granted.

'You must both have had fun.'

'We did,' she said. 'Especially in the Broadstairs days.'

Should she tell him other things? Her fears about Stella Davidge? About Angela? Or should she think round these things some more? Take another look at that old file first?

Kenworthy was an old hand at spotting hesitation.

'There's something else, isn't there?'

'But probably nothing in it. I keep thinking of a friend that my mother made, just before we married.'

'A man?'

'A woman. I've no reason to think anything sinister about her. There was something a little sickening about it. I don't know quite what it was. They were so thick together—as if they were soul-mates who'd spent a lifetime waiting for each other. And they worked on each other. For one thing, they drank too much. And that wasn't one of my mother's habits—not a regular one, anyway.'

She tried to smile it away apologetically.

'You must excuse me. Anyone would think I'd spent my life being jealous of anyone who wanted my mother's company. But she sometimes got herself tied up with some pretty poor types, in my estimation. Then she'd have the problem of sloughing them off.'

'And she didn't slough this one off?'

'She hadn't before we left for Spain. I spotted her in church at our wedding.'

'Her name?'

'Angela. Angela Hallam. But I don't know whether that was her married name or what her personal arrangements were.'

'Can you describe her?'

'I'd say she was a few years older than my mother, doing her best to look several years younger. A well-preserved figure, but her make-up was crucial, if her age wasn't to show.'

'You didn't like her at all?'

'She was so knowing. She looked at me as if she despised me—while at the same time professing open-hearted friendship. She was utterly cynical about Howard and me and our—'

She was going to say *decency*, but said *optimism* instead.

'What did she and your mother do together?'

'I don't know, not really. Nothing very original. Ate out. Drank—both out and at home. They didn't talk to me about their outings.'

'And there's something else worrying you, isn't there?'

'Like Angela Hallam, it could be nothing.'

'We have nothing to go on, except things that might be nothing.'

'Just before our honeymoon, I caught sight of a file. It wasn't a job I was working on—it just caught my eye while I was looking for something else. I glanced through it, that was all—and I haven't been back in the office since.'

'It worried you?'

'It struck me. It was about a girl who left home after having a baby. She was just about the right age to have been Mother. But that goes for thousands of others, I know.'

'Tell me more about this one.'

'I'd like to refresh my mind first, look at the file again.'

'Do that, then—then bring it straight up to me, even if you find you've cooled off about it. What sector are you on at the moment?

'Nineteen-thirty-nine, March to September. But I sometimes get off course and follow things up. I start reading things that shouldn't concern me.'

'We all do that. It can be fatal. And sometimes very informative. Nobody's got to nineteen-fifty-eight to 'sixty-three yet, have they?'

'No, Mr Kenworthy—not yet allocated.'

'Move over to that bracket. That assignment ought to keep
a bright young lady occupied for a week or two. Nineteen-
thirty-nine can wait on ice—there aren't many of those
wrong 'uns still around. And if you find anything, you have
direct access to me. Don't talk on the open phone if you don't
want to. Come up and see me.'

She could hear traffic outside, someone hooting for his own
satisfaction at a driver slow to pull out from a junction.

'You know what triggers you are looking for?'

'Birth certificates?'

'That would be jam on it. You won't be so lucky. And
remember that not all missing persons get on our files.
Sometimes even missing children are not reported. Sometimes people abscond, and nobody wants them back anyway.
But I don't want to feed you too many ideas. They might
hamstring you. Follow your nose. You'll find things.'

She might light on something particularly nasty, and it
might be her own self that she'd go on to discover. The
interview was over. As soon as she had left him, Kenworthy
ran his eye speedily over the few bits of paper that had come
in to him this morning. He appended notes to send them on
their way, then lit his pipe.

Then he asked switchboard to get him a Lancashire
number.

CHAPTER 8

They had never intended to live with Howard's parents. But
there was no question of taking over Jean Cossey's flat,
even though the lease could easily have been transferred.
Anne could not have borne that. No one suggested she
should.

The house that she and Howard were waiting to move into
had been victim of every possible form of contractor's

trouble, from labour disputes to non-flow of capital. They had already postponed their wedding date once, and could not put off guests and the givers of presents again. Nor could they jockey about trying to co-ordinate another set of leave patterns. They did not want to wait, anyway.

In close prospect, Anne was uneasy about living with the Lawsons. For all their meticulous kindness, her parents-in-law lived beyond an unfamiliar chasm. She felt the undertow beneath their faultless code of No Comment. No criticism was voiced: yet she felt perpetually on the brink of it. And the Lawsons' tastes and thoughts were not hers. They started introducing her to a social set with whom she had nothing in common. True, she would be out of the house during commuting hours—but there would be no hope that Howard's shifts would often coincide with hers. He would often be on duty at weekends, and the gaping void of Sundays horrified her. Now there even seemed to have been a certain cosiness in the years with her mother, a snugness more easy to remember than their bickerings.

Then something else happened. She discovered that she was pregnant.

The man whom Kenworthy rang in Lancashire was Superintendent Bartram, with whom he had once worked on a provincial case. Bartram was a joker, a man under compulsion to say something funny as a prelude to every statement he made. Four times out of five it was worth at least a smile, and at least that unified his audience. Bartram was a good copper. Because there are other things to being a good copper, besides the number of villains that you nick. It is sometimes worth spending time with people—time that your superiors might consider wasted, if they knew about it. Bartram was a born chatter-up of strangers—and he owed Kenworthy a favour. Bartram had been catching an unfair ration of cloud-shadow when Kenworthy had been wished on him. They had set about looking at things together in a

civilized manner, and Kenworthy had left him with the
bonus of a cleared case.

'Bartram?'

'What can we do for you this time, you damned old rogue?
Spot of cat burglary up Blackpool Tower?'

'One of those jobs that they might not wear if I try to pass it
through the bosses. Come to that, I'm not supposed to be on
the case myself.'

'That's pickle on the side of the plate.'

'Slodden-le-Woods. Eighteen years ago.'

Slodden was not on Bartram's patch. He might or might
not have difficulty making inquiries there. It depended on
the liver of the Slodden incumbent.

'No problem,' Bartram said. 'They have long memories in
Slodden.'

'They'll need them. I want to know about a girl who was
calling herself Jean Carter at the time. She came to Slodden
in 1963 with a four-year-old child, worked somewhere in a
mucky factory. The child, name of Anne, was minded by a
woman called Gregory till she was old enough for school.
They left in 'sixty-six.'

'Anything else about them?'

'Mother got murdered a few days ago. Bath-water too hot.
You do read the papers?'

'What do you want me to find out?'

'Everything.'

'As good as done. You know where to come when it's
service you want.'

There was another source of information that Kenworthy
wished was already computerized: the movements in and out
of Her Majesty's Prisons over the years. Who had been
released in the late spring of 1963—and had then traced Jean
Cossey to Broadstairs, thus sending her fleeing up to
Slodden? Who had gone down again in 1966, leaving Jean
Cossey free to take Anne to live in London? Who had been set

at liberty again not so very long before Anne's wedding, and had succeeded in locating Jean Cossey?

There were too many of them. They came and went to and from too many places. It had to be another case for decidedly human sampling—for running the naked eye down the columns here and there. People were accustomed to receiving from Kenworthy short-notice demands which they did not see why he should need. He limited himself in the first instance to release records from top security wings. They were better documented, and Mr Camel-Leopard had probably qualified for high-class treatment.

And what were the previous aliases of Angela Hallam? Kenworthy saw no way of coming to immediate grips with that.

The early stages of Anne Lawson's pregnancy were troublesome. Her euphemistically styled morning sickness prolonged itself for hours after unfaced breakfasts. She suffered vertigos, nauseas and nervous deficiency at random hours of day. She became difficult to get on with, and those who had had no experience of getting on with her at normal times were misled into a wrong impression of her temperament. She was snappish, she knew that she was being snappish, and it seemed that she could do nothing to organize herself. Her mother-in-law had never learned how to be passively kind. She did not know how to keep her kindness in the background. When at a loss, she had a tendency to become fussy. She asked Anne whether she wanted a girl or a boy. Anne held strong views about that question. If she expressed a preference now, she might have to imply disappointment later on. She answered in a tone that conveyed her bile rather than her meaning.

'I only asked,' Mrs Lawson Senior said.

Slodden-le-Woods was one of those cotton towns that might still serve as a text-book illustration of the Industrial Revolution—even though it had long since lost its cotton. The first mill had been built in a valley bottom, where a chilly brook from off the Pennines had driven a water-wheel. The newest mill, 1908, had portentous copper turrets and prosperous streaky-bacon brick-work. There was also coal in the vicinity, which had added slag to the contours. There was a dyeworks, with an effluent that sometimes stank. The miners, spinners and dyers had been incarcerated in terraces that clung in steep geometry to the flanks of narrow valleys. Now every front room had colour TV, and many of them video-recorders as well.

There were reasons why Bartram would have preferred to have been asked to go free-booting elsewhere than in Slodden. They boiled down to the hubris of Bill Smalley. Bartram and Smalley had risen to be Superintendents up different crevices. Bartram had used imagination and diplomacy, was socially amusing, had flair. Smalley had always played safe, stayed in line. He was mentally myopic, and like many men of close vision, he could be obsessed by trivialities.

Bartram went to Smalley and said he wanted to make a small inquiry on his manor. He did not confess that he was doing it on a rest day. He did not hint that this was a favour to the Met that had not gone through the books. He had jested his way out of less petty infringements than this in his time.

He called first at the school that Anne had most probably attended, but here he was frustrated. There had been a complete turnover of staff since Anne's day. The attendance registers for that far-off period had been sent to the Education Department. Bartram lost half a day, finding the right clerk to rummage in the right cabinet. It was late afternoon before he got back to Slodden.

No. 39, Darwen Road, had changed owners twice since the Cossey-Carters had lodged there. It was one of a long climbing row that had been built for £300 each just before the First World War; its present owner had borrowed £9000 for it just before becoming unemployed last year. His wife had given up trying to captivate him, but there was enough of her eighteen-year-old sexiness left within her twenty-four-year-old frame to suggest how they had come to get married. And no, they knew nothing at all about the last occupant but one of their house.

Bartram went to the neighbours. He found several who remembered Alice Stanford, who had died in No. 39. She had been a respectable weaver's widow who had let her spare bedroom. And yes—people remembered the Carters, mother and daughter. Old Alice would not have turned away an unmarried mother and child.

And, people had to say, Alice Stanford had not been let down. Jean Carter had proved a decent, sober, hard-working young woman, whose daughter was more than a credit to her. Oh, they had all had their doubts at first. Mrs Carter—she called herself Mrs, but Darwen Road had not been taken in by that—had looked like a woman with a roving eye. There had at one time been something between her and one of the foremen at Ormsby and Gregg's, where she worked. Stan Boulter, a married man. But nothing had come of it. Mrs Carter had somehow extricated herself from something that would have spelled only trouble, and had gone on to conduct herself quietly for many months. She had even managed to hold on at Ormsby's without getting aggro from Boulter.

Ormsby and Gregg's had had the receiver in eighteen months ago. The gates were padlocked. Someone had daubed anti-Thatcher signs over the warehouse door. Was it worth digging out Stan Boulter?

Then Bartram struck ringing ore. He found Anne Carter-Cossey's babysitter. And the moment he set eyes on Nellie Gregory, he knew he was on the road.

CHAPTER 9

Anne Lawson dreamed again, but this time with a difference. Again they were the Hobbema trees, their tall trunks stark and familiar. As always, their branches were menacing, knowing. It was an irrational adjective to use of the branches of a tree—but that was the impression that they always gave her. They knew who she was, and where she was, and what she was doing here, and what was going to happen to her next. And she knew none of these things. They were a sort of personified accusation—but she did not know what they were accusing her of.

As she got out of bed, sick before racing for her commuter train, she felt as if she had been deprived of sleep all night.

Nellie Gregory was on the sixty mark. Twenty years ago she must have been an even more uncompromising woman, even more confident and careless in her snap judgements. The threshold of old age might have quietened her down somewhat. Perhaps she even felt the cautionary influence of a man who introduced himself frankly as an off-duty police superintendent. But she did not much care about the ranks and precedences of men. She lavishly proclaimed the contrary. She was a woman who had always lived by announcing a reputation that she then had to live up to.

She believed in speaking her mind (she said) and her mind, when spoken, was exclusively destructive. She tore down idols: and many and varied were the things that were idols to Nellie Gregory. Nearly every word she spoke was a slander of someone or other. She attacked everyone who departed from her norms. The difficulty lay in establishing what her norms were.

Bartram did not take long to decide that Anne Carter must

have detested every hour that she spent in Nellie Gregory's care. It came out early in the conversation that there had been a certain refinement—a sensitivity—about Anne, a precocious fastidiousness of speech, the beginnings of orthodoxy in English grammar, perhaps—and firm home-training in matters of elementary hygiene. Nellie Gregory was not an unclean woman, but her closest cronies would not have called her fussy. There had been things about Anne that had been different—and they were suspect in Nellie Gregory's eyes. In a bigger girl, they would have been the brand-marks of an intolerable superiority. And Nellie Gregory was not blind to the irony that this was the child of a woman who, somewhere down her line, had come off the rails. Nellie would not say a word of that to the child; but the child would know that she was thinking something nasty. Sometimes Nellie would be overloud in her remarks to other people. And she was not beyond talking to herself, if that was the only way of ridding her system of poison.

Not that she was an unkind woman. Bluntness had never hurt her, and if it hurt other people, it was a pity they had not grown out of such softness. She thought scathing thoughts about Jean Carter's past moral turpitude; but if Jean Carter had stood in visible material need, Nellie Gregory would have done what she could for her. Bartram was able to meet her mentality three-quarters of the way. He spoke the language of women like Nellie Gregory.

'Pretty snooty bloody lot down this end of Paradise Alley, are they, then?'

She waited for him to answer his own riddle.

'I just heard her at Number Ten call a dog-turd a visiting card.'

'Oh, her—'

'You used to mind a little girl—oh, years ago—eighteen, to give chapter and verse.'

'I've looked after a lot in my time.'

'Some of them must stand out. Like Anne Carter?'

'Anne Carter?'

'Mother used to lodge with Alice Stanford. Worked at Ormsby's.'

'I remember. She used to make me laugh. The little girl, I mean. Very proper. Used to look at me with such serious eyes. She couldn't make me out.'

'And what about her mother? Could you make her out?'

'Mrs Carter? Or should it have been Miss Carter? Miss Something-or-other, anyway. Not one of us. I don't know what it was about her. Didn't exactly give herself airs. She couldn't, hardly, working in the finishing-shop at Ormsby's, could she? But she wasn't one you ever got to know. Folks don't care for secrets, round here. You only get back from folks what you give them.'

'Maybe Mrs Carter didn't want anything back.'

'She had something on her mind. She'd come unstuck once, that's for sure. We're not a prying lot, round here, but a lot of people would have given their ears to know how, when—and by who.'

'There's folks as still would,' Bartram said.

Nellie Gregory was smart enough to know that he was not here for gossip. Men like Bartram did not come slumming for kicks.

'I don't know what else I can tell you,' she said, fishing for a lead.

'Had she men friends?'

'Once or twice. She hung about the foreman's office at the works at one time. Stan Boulter knew how to make women feel sorry for him. Some women.'

'Is Stan Boulter still about?'

'Telling the angels that his wife didn't understand him. What's she done, this Mrs Carter?'

'That's what I hoped someone in Slodden might tell me.'

'I don't know what you take us for in Slodden. We know how to mind our own business, here. Mind you, I used to look at her sometimes and think to myself: you're going to get more than you've bargained for, one of these days, my young lady.'

'Why was that, then?'

'She had that look about her.'

Bartram knew what she meant, though she could not express it. The moment women like Nellie Gregory started trying to analyse their thoughts, their thoughts ceased to be useful.

'Coming like she did from nowhere. Then off again, two-three years later, not so much as dropping in to say goodbye.'

When Jean Carter had seen the light go green for leaving Slodden, she had not been slow about shaking the dust off.

'I didn't go much for her friends, either,' Nellie Gregory said.

'Any particular friend in mind?'

'There was a Mrs Beecham, over up Barleyfields. A Gwen Beecham.'

Barleyfields. A spec-built estate, intended in the 'fifties to bring middle-class money over to the greener side of Slodden. It had petered out after an avenue and a half. You could still just about see where they'd laid out future roads and closes.

'No bottle,' Nellie Gregory said, writing off Gwen Beecham in a phrase of decisive dismissal. 'If Mrs Carter gave herself airs, you thought just now and then there might possibly once have been something behind them—especially when you looked at her kid. But Gwen Beecham was never owt but froth. Damn it, I saw her once in Madgwick's chemists, buying herself a packet for a foam-bath. What does anyone in Slodden want with a foam-bath?'

You had to be close to Nellie Gregory's mind to catch the full flavour of her condemnations.

'It was Mrs Beecham who came round to fix up about the kid coming here. I reckon it was her found Alice Stanford for them. I dare say it was Gwen Beecham who put in a word for her at Ormsby's. And she's another who's come undone at the seams. Divorced,' Nellie Gregory said, shredding the woman's character into its ultimate ribbons.

'Maybe she didn't get on with her old man,' Bartram suggested.

'There's no telling what that poor bugger had to put up with.'

Foam-baths, perhaps—

'Gone away, has she?'

'Three-four years ago.'

'Bugger it! Folks are slipping away from me in all directions. Well, I mustn't take up any more of your precious time.'

CHAPTER 10

It seemed that nothing could save Mrs Lawson and Anne from misunderstandings. Every issue that arose had its dangers. Mrs Lawson was already knitting frenetically, and seemed to have an inexhaustible supply of patterns that ought to be in some costume museum. She could not be blind to Anne's lack of enthusiasm. Then she produced the Baby Book on whose doctrines Howard had been raised, and that led to a discussion of Howard's character in which they did not seem to be talking about the same man.

The next day, Sunday, Howard was actually home. And the elder Lawsons announced that they were going out visiting for the day, presumably a noble gesture to give the young people time to themselves.

But the young people seemed unable to recapture any magic. Anne felt so unsteady when she tried to stand on her legs that she could not even face the thin, milkless tea that Howard brought up to her. She pretended to sleep for the next hour and a half, and when she finally came downstairs, Howard was lost to her, in filthy mid-stream of reorganizing his father's garage, a job he had been promising to do for months.

At the lunch table she could only pick at her plate. And he told her that he had a surprise in store for her tomorrow. How would she like a day in Broadstairs? Not, he added, that they had much choice.

'No choice? For one thing, I'm working tomorrow.'

'That's all fixed.'

'Fixed, is it? So would you mind telling me how much else in my life has been fixed?'

'It will do you good, a breath of sea air. And for me it's duty—the sort of outing that doesn't fall in one's lap every day.'

'I think I might have been asked. Broadstairs! Are you trying to break my heart?'

'It's in the best of causes. And in any case, it's orders.'

'Whose orders?'

'Shiner's.'

'And since when have I been working for Shiner?'

'That's neither here nor there. I would have thought, for the sake of finding out who killed your mother—'

Outburst: the boiling over of the pot.

'What does it matter who killed her? Will that bring her back?'

Was she so far gone that she couldn't steer clear of a cliché like that?

'What's the point of dredging? What do you expect me to find for you in Broadstairs? I haven't set foot there since I was four.'

Her mother, in fact, had always refused to the point of anger to go back to the Thanet coast. At the age of thirteen or fourteen, Anne had had twisted thoughts about what might be so horrifying to her mother in the thought of Broadstairs.

'Well, point number one is that I'm not an element in anybody's brief. Point number two is that I wouldn't even be able to find the house we lived in.'

'That is the point. If you saw it again, you might remember.'

'I don't want to remember anything.'

'In that case, I'll let Shiner know. He said not to press you. I'll go on my own—if he thinks that's worth while.'

Her nausea was so bad that she closed her eyes and felt as if she were about to fall over backwards.

'Are you all right, darling?'

'Of course I'm not all right.'

Kenworthy walked round the end of the counter of the radio parts shop that Lionel Friedman's son ran in Warren Street. The onset of video had put a new line of goods in the window. Terry Friedman did not know Kenworthy, and tried to put his anything but formidable body in the way.

'Law,' Kenworthy said.

'You'll stay on that side, unless you've a warrant. I was gone over last week—and found clean.'

'I'm not looking for dirty pictures. I want a word with your dad.'

'You ask first, then. Who are you?'

'Kenworthy.'

Only seconds later, young Friedman—he was not far under fifty—was back, sullen, because his father suddenly wanted a red mat laid out for the fuzz.

Lionel Friedman was an old man whose years had taken flesh off a frame not too well endowed with it in the first place. It was twenty years, at Kenworthy's round guess, since Lionel had last done anything significantly unlawful. He'd done porridge—not a lot—and the time had come, in sight of his pension, when he had decided that he was too old to face another basinful. He had disposed of his plates and presses and some, though not all, of his engraving tools. Kenworthy thought he knew who had bought them—but that information was not for direct question. And in retirement, old Lionel had lost neither his eye nor his willingness to learn. He was not by nature an idle man. At the moment he was doing something with a soldering iron to the circuit of a pocket calculator, the specification spread out on the bench in front of him.

'Unexpected pleasure, Mr Kenworthy.'

'Unexpected necessity, Mr Friedman.'

'You know I've been retired a long time now, Mr Kenworthy.'

'Except for very special favours for very special clients.'

'Off-target, Mr Kenworthy. I'd have to be bloody desperate to risk the sort of company they put me with last time.'

He set down his soldering iron.

'I mean, I was a professional. You've got to admit that. They slammed me up with a couple of tea-leaves. From south of the river.'

Kenworthy looked round for a chair, had to make do with a stool.

'Just pulling your pisser, Lionel. If I wasn't ready to believe every word you say, I wouldn't waste my time coming here. I need help.'

'Anything I know is twenty years old.'

'I'll split the difference. I only want to go back six. Birth certificates.'

And Friedman laughed—as near to a belly-laugh as a man with no belly could manage.

'Never touched them. You won't find many who would. They take a narrow view of anything connected with that sort of caper—ladle out the gruel with a JCB.'

'They weren't too ungenerous with those cheque-books you did, were they?'

'Don't be unkind, Mr K—I had a lot of expenses at the time.'

'I'm sorry—I ought to have asked—how is Nora?'

'Never looked back since she had her bits and pieces out.'

'She must have been glad to see you settle down. Now—birth certificates. You never handled them. I believe you.

But suppose—just suppose—you'd had some big domestic expense in your youth. You needed a birth certificate blank for a top-paying client. You'd have known where to get one?'

'Very expensive,' Friedman said. 'Like paying corkage on your own South African plonk in the Dorchester. There was one man. You know him. A loner.'

Friedman looked down at the wiring of the calculator as if it were calling him.

'So you won't need me to say his name.'

'I knew a chap who once supplied Giro cheques for a supplementary benefits hand-out. But the job had to be called off.'

But Lionel Friedman was too old a hand to be caught by a superior-knowledge ploy.

'That would have been a mug's game,' he said, switching on his iron. 'Don't think I'm trying to hurry you. It takes this thing a bit to warm up.'

'You disappoint me, Lionel.'

'When I pulled out, Mr Kenworthy, I pulled out from both sides. I don't fancy losing my looks to a chivver. I have Nora to think about.'

'OK, I'll try elsewhere. But if anyone should drop in in the next day or two and whip you round to Victoria Street for questioning about video-tapes, try asking for me. I might have an ounce or two I can throw into the balance.'

Friedman tested his iron with a moistened fingertip.

'You're a pack of bastards, you lot.'

'Listen, Lionel—six years ago, a young woman—'

'I don't see that it concerns me.'

'It concerns me. Because a few days ago this woman died. She died in her bath. The mains supply had somewhere got mixed up in the water. I expect you'll have heard about it.'

'And you think I can tell you anything about that?'

'It all turns on birth certificates—six years ago.'

'She didn't get them off me.'

'There aren't many others she could have got them off.

And what defeats me is how would she have known where to go.'

'I was out of the game by then. Out of all the games.'

Kenworthy got up and wandered a few paces about the grubby little workshop.

'I gather one of our DI's has started showing an interest in your son.'

There was a bloodshot spot in one of Lionel's eyes.

'You'll get nothing out of me that way. There's nothing to be got out.'

'Spicer's Roller Towel Service—that's how you're all taking delivery, I hear. Not dirty tapes—just pirated ones, Lionel. A word in your ear: there's a drive on.'

'They've been and done us over. There was nothing for them to find.'

'There will be next time.'

Both Friedman and Kenworthy knew that evidence could sometimes be where a DI wanted it.

'All right. But it wouldn't do for him to know that I'd sent you to him. Let me go and see him first. Let me go and explain to him, Mr Kenworthy. Because it's Swannee Foster.'

He said the name as if he expected it to be the universal passport to special treatment.

'How soon can you get to him, Lionel?'

'Tomorrow. If you could put off going there until after four o'clock tomorrow afternoon, Mr Kenworthy—'

'I'll be there at five past,' Kenworthy said.

CHAPTER 11

Howard had not rung the DI. If he had felt diffident about disturbing him at home on a weeknight, he felt even less keen on a Sunday. Tomorrow morning he would report that Anne had wakened up more than usually under the weather. But on the Monday morning she was up before he was, had made him tea. Howard's mother was also padding about in the kitchen, in a green quilted housecoat.

Anne was determined to fight her malaise down. She was going to Broadstairs with Howard today if her sickness blinded her. Howard was shaken by how ghastly she looked.

'They're not expecting you in today, anyway,' he said.

'I'm not going in. I'm coming with you.'

No one was going to say that she was a spoke in his wheel. She made it to the passenger seat of their G registration Cortina. Once they had started moving, she told herself, once she had wound down the window, once there was cool, non-smelling air on her face, she'd feel better. This thing came and went in phases.

'Stop somewhere and buy me some mints—*Glacier* mints.'

They were the only thing she felt safe to have in her mouth. Rain started at Sittingbourne, one of those grey, sea-mist drizzles that sometimes hang over the Thames estuary like a damp Shetland blanket. She had never even known their postal address in Broadstairs, but she had a vague hope that she might recognize their road when she saw it. It had been a long, straight road, leading down to the sea from a highway where red buses ran.

'You talked about a beach with a natural arch,' Howard said. 'If we could find that, things might start coming back to you. And this sort of weather often changes when the tide turns.'

'What am I supposed to be looking for?' she asked, as they drove out of Whitstable. They had left the main road to look for a coffee. She had nibbled without after-effect at a Kitkat.

'Maybe some shop you used to go in with your mother. That might take us to a face that you recognize—someone we could ask—someone who might remember more than you do. We can surely find your kindergarten.'

They came in along the Margate sea-front, past the Royal

Sea Bathing Hospital and Dreamland. She twisted in her seat as they approached the Harbour.

'That must be where I had the ice-cream with the sparklers. The name looks Italian. But I don't remember any of this.'

It was not clear whether the tide had turned or not, but there was no change in the weather. Putting Cliftonville behind them, they started looking at beaches. It was not long before they came upon the arch. And it did lead down to an enclosed cove, which a storm had littered with great boulders of chalk.

'Do you remember this?'

'It's no use saying I do. And what this beach needs is a fringe of palms.'

Leading up from the green clifftop were three parallel avenues: large pre-Second World War villas at the lower end, earlier houses in the upper reaches.

'I've got a feeling the school was in one of those half-timbered places.'

They walked past them all, and found no kindergarten.

'Are you sure you feel up to this?'

'I'm enjoying it. I like the quiet. I even like the cold air.'

And that was true. This was one of her better hours. He went to the door of one of the large houses to ask, learned that the school had ceased to exist more than ten years ago. The proprietress-headmistress had died. She had operated in a double-fronted mock-Tudor now called Channel Winds.

Anne looked in at the gateway. Three enormous bay windows must have belonged to the main schoolroom. Where had they been let out to play? She had a memory of a sandpit, a climbing-frame. There were no signs of climbing-frame or sandpit here.

'Where's it all gone? I was happy here. Now it's as if I'd never seen it before. It's depressing.'

'It's a depressing day.'

Behind them the sea was a continuous surge, even the

cliff-edge merging into mist fifty yards away.

'But you know what,' Anne said. 'I could find my way home from here.'

Home: the word fell naturally from her lips. It was the first time she had used it in this context.

'Not by taking thought, as the Bible puts it. But by letting my footsteps take me.'

'Let them take you, then.'

She walked a pace ahead of him; it was her expedition now. They took a side-road, between garden hedges, into the second of the avenues. Then a similar link-road brought them into the third road. The sea was both behind them now and in front. They were on the very tip of Thanet, of Kent, of England. Behind the houses opposite must be the cornfields she had seen from her bedroom window. A foghorn was sounding on a distant sandbank.

'It must have been one of these.'

They had reached a row of less prosperous houses— though they were far from impoverished. There were eight of them in a terrace, three-storeyed, with mansard windows. They had small front gardens, in one of them a honeysuckle hedge, clematis climbing a porch, paintwork in good trim.

'I think it was one of those in the middle.'

'We'll walk slowly past. Look at the patterns of the doors. Some of them have stained-glass panels. One of those might remind you.'

But they roused nothing in her. An elderly man came out of one of the doors, hobbled to his gate, leaned out bending forward from the base of his spine.

'Mr Okapi!'

The man turned to look her full in the face with damp, irritable eyes; no recognition—only the one-way resentment of senility. He turned and went into the house without speaking.

'Another of your menagerie?'

'Out of the same picture-book. I used to call him that. He

used to wear a pullover with a band of stripes round the bottom. He liked being called Mr Okapi. We were good friends.'

'He's probably living with a son or daughter.'

A woman appeared at the door of the house.

'Mrs Harrington?'

Anne remembered. Mrs Harrington remembered. She called her Anne Cresswell. There was a scene of incredulous joy. The woman was comfortably middle-aged, uninhibitedly sentimental.

'You used to collect dandelion leaves for my rabbit. Your mother always looked so unbelievably young to have had you. Then, not a word of warning, a taxi at the gate, and you were away. My father—a stroke—but he knew you when you called him Mr Okapi. He came in and said—'

Mrs Harrington even had some badly shot box-camera snapshots of Anne and her mother. Jean Cossey looked singularly uncare-ridden.

'Was there anything else that struck you about that sudden departure?' Howard asked.

The question and its tone puzzled Mrs Harrington.

'What sort of thing would you call striking?'

'Had there been, for example, any unusual callers?'

'I'm not a peeper round curtain edges.'

'I'm sure you're not. But wasn't there something of a mystery about the whole thing? If you'd seen anything odd, you'd have talked about it among yourselves, wouldn't you?'

Anne took no part in this. She went over and put a hand on Mrs Harrington's father's arm.

'I thought you didn't know me outside just now, Mr Okapi.'

'He hasn't found his voice properly,' Mrs Harrington said. 'He's shy about talking to strangers. He says he croaks like a frog. His voice is all right, isn't it? Tell him his voice is fine, Anne.'

Howard came back to his questioning.

'You're asking me what sort of friends Mrs Cresswell made? There was nothing wrong in her looking for a father for her child, was there? And it wasn't to her discredit if she gave them their cards when they did not come up to scratch.'

'Was there anyone in particular?' Howard asked. 'Was there any friendship that lasted longer than the rest? Was there any that really looked as if it was going to come off? Or any that packed up more spectacularly than the rest?'

'I don't know why you are getting on to me like this.'

And Anne intervened.

'Don't bully poor Mrs Harrington. Don't you think we ought to tell her why we are really here? She only knew Mother as Cresswell. What about Cossey? A name you'll perhaps have heard in the news, Mrs Harrington.'

Mrs Harrington was slow to associate Jean Cresswell with the new identity. The revelation bewildered and distressed her. But it did not, could not, lead her on to tell them anything useful.

'All I remember is a very happy mother, laughing most of the time. It's a good thing, I always say, that we don't know in advance what life holds for us.'

After they had left the avenue, Howard went on to something more positive. They went the round of the Broadstairs estate agents, of whom there were few enough for this to be a feasible proposition. In eighteen years there had been many new faces, but he came across one staid old firm whose proprietor, an elderly man called Stopford, talked as if he had been deprived of an audience for years. He was the sort of man who never destroyed a file, and when Howard mentioned the house they had just pinpointed, he recognized it immediately as a property that had been through his hands more than once.

'In nineteen-sixty-three, you say? That should not surpass the wit of man.'

He established Jean Cresswell's as a long furnished letting, twelve months from November, 1962. Rent had been paid in advance and £150 deposited for damage and contingencies. Stopford had kept every item of correspondence, including the letter of initial inquiry, in handwriting that was undoubtedly Anne's mother's. The address from which she had written was c/o Agnew, Waterman's Cottage, Spurlsby Drove, Lincs.

It was a matter of routine to ask the Lincolnshire police for a discreet fill-in on Waterman's Cottage. In the event, discretion was superfluous, since the row of three of which the Agnews' home had been one had been converted into a single dwelling eight years ago, and was now occupied by a professor emeritus of political economy. The Agnews, an elderly couple even in Jean Cossey's youth, had died: it was their tenure of the cottage that had for a long time held up the sale of the place: the other two houses had been crumbling vacant for years.

What the rural CID did not include in their report—because they knew nothing of Anne Lawson's dreams—was that Spurlsby Drove was a grassy, sandy track lined by tall trees. As one entered it, one saw a large house framed by a proscenium arch of high branches.

CHAPTER 12

Anne was not fit to go to her office the morning after the Broadstairs trip. This was obvious to Howard, who was frightened by the state he saw her in today. He urged her to call in the doctor. But between ten o'clock and half past, she risked standing on her feet and came down to the kitchen to see if she could find something bland enough to try to eat.

Mrs Lawson was in astringent mood—that was how Anne interpreted it. She seemed to be telling her daughter-in-law to pull herself together. She reminisced about her own single pregnancy, how she had carried Howard with little noticeable inconvenience or discomfort. Moreover, Mrs Lawson felt that yesterday's gadding about in Kent—those were the words that she was so ill-advised as to use—had been, to say the least, imprudent.

'That was *work*,' Anne told her, hitting back vigorously. And that led to a discussion—not their first—as to whether a woman ought to go out to work when her husband was compelled to keep such irregular hours as Howard. The two women did not speak from the same standpoint.

'As for earning, I don't see the necessity for it in your case. You need have virtually no overheads while you're living with us. Howard's father and I—'

Anne thought that this silly battle had already been fought and won. She had insisted on paying their share of the housekeeping. She tartly reminded her mother-in-law of that. She had found the remnants of a barley cordial that she thought she fancied, but as it tasted old and stale, she emptied her glass down the sink. Mrs Lawson took the gesture as petulance. She upbraided Anne. Anne came back in fury.

'Howard and I will move over to our house as soon as it is fit to camp out in. I am now leaving for work, and if I don't come home this evening, it will be because I have found somewhere temporary to live.'

Mrs Lawson was desolate. What had she said? she later asked Howard. Anyone could see that the child was unwell— but she ought to make some effort to control herself.

The room in which Anne worked was heavy with cigarette-smoke, but there was a limit to the addictions that a woman could ask her colleagues to abjure. Cigarette-smoke turned her stomach over; the sight of yet someone else lighting up was of itself enough to set her off again. Kenworthy came down into the office to check on something. His pipe was seldom out of his mouth. He was smoking it now. He put a match to the bowl.

'I thought you weren't coming in today.'

She fanned the blue cloud away from her face. There were eyes in the room staring at her. One did not treat Kenworthy like that.

'I felt better after the first hour. Maybe I can stick it out—if I don't end up kippered.'

He made no comment, turned to speak to the clerk he had come to see. There was silence at the other desks. Kenworthy had never played the martinet in this department, though a reputation had preceded him. Anne applied herself with what concentration she could muster to her stack of files.

She had already sent up to Kenworthy the one about Stella Davidge, but he had so far not disclosed his reaction to it. He must surely consider it irrelevant. Or if he wanted it followed up, he might have delegated it to someone who had not even started on it yet. Perhaps he had not even got round to reading it himself.

In 1959, in the heart of Metroland, in Northwood Hills, Stella Davidge, a sixteen-year-old schoolgirl, had become pregnant. Good family, good home. Her father was an assessor of fire insurance. There had been nothing specific on file about the mother, but Anne thought she could imagine her: Metroland, a senior insurance man's wife. Nothing at all was known about the father of the baby; suspicions were always less than helpful. Stella Davidge had shown remarkable firmness in the way she had kept her lips sealed. But she had not been shrewd in her practical handling of her problem. She had kept her condition dark until well after the deadline for an abortion: fear of facing up to the *brouhaha* no doubt. Her parents had not had an inkling. Not an inkling? Hadn't her mother ever seen her in the bath? Oh, she admitted that she thought that her daughter was getting plumpish, but she had put that down to puppy-fat.

Of course, the parents had been crushingly kind, magnificently forgiving—but without any shred of real understanding. After the foundation-rocking shock came the

master-plan: adoption, change of residence. For years the
Davidges had talked about moving up into leafy Bucks:
Missenden or Wendover. Stella could go to a new school.
Her undoubted university prospects would not be in jeop-
ardy. The trouble was, Stella somehow got the absurd notion
into her hopelessly immature brain that she wanted to keep
the child. How, keep it? Where? With what support? And
with what prospects for either of them?

Private nursing home. Battery of persuaders. The GP was
clearly being pressurized by the parents. Yet one particular
welfare officer was obtusely on the girl's side. After ten days,
Stella and child disappeared. The Met alerted all nets.
Private eyes made fat fees without results. Davidge called in
the Salvation Army—magnificent reputation in such cases—
made a hefty donation. No trace.

The file was left open. It had not been reviewed for years.
Why should it be, keeping company as it was with thousands
of others?

So could Anne's true maiden name have been Davidge? Of
course, there were some details that would have to be made
to fit. It would mean that Jean Cossey had never told the
truth about her age. And hadn't everyone said what a young
mother she seemed? Had she been Stella Davidge? And if so,
what sort of chromosomes did that give Anne? What sort of
child had Stella Davidge been? Irresponsible? Precocious?
Nympho? Or just damned unlucky—and stubborn?

Come to that, how much of the nympho had always been
trying to get out of Jean Cossey? There had been some stories
about her mother that Anne had never told Howard—
hadn't, latterly, cared to remind herself of. In the romantic
innocence of childhood, Anne had sometimes felt that her
mother was besotted by men. If she hadn't got a man-friend
at any given moment, she was either looking at one or for one.
Some of those she seemed to think were heroes were dead-
beat grotty—even in the eyes of a fatherless child.

There had been an incident that Anne had succeeded in

forgetting, but that jack-in-the-boxed disgustingly into memory from time to time. It had been in Slodden, just before they had mercifully pulled out of Lancashire. She was seven. Their old landlady had gone into hospital for a few days for tests: something said in whispers about her bowels. Jean Carter's friend of the moment was a salesman called Arthur, who came from the other side of Bolton and had an estate car with women's dresses crowded on hangers in the back. Anne knew, with the indeceivable sagacity of childhood, that a lot of complicated pretence was going on to hide the fact that Arthur was going to stay the night. The sounds of doors and of feet on stairs had to be elaborately concealed from the neighbours.

During the night, Anne heard disconcerting noises through the wall. It was as if her mother were tossing and turning sleepless on the ancient springs of her bed. And she seemed to be groaning with pain at every exhalation from her lungs. Thinking her mother ill, the child pattered along the cold linoleum, out on to the landing, to tap on the door. After a delay, with an upheaving creak from the bed, her mother opened up to her.

'What is it? Why are you out of bed?'

After she had been tucked up again, Anne heard a giggle in the next room. It was that giggle that she resented most of all—resented it all the more later, when she knew beyond doubt what it had all been about. It was all so furtive, so unclean. Well: hadn't she and Howard had to be furtive, too, once or twice, in their early days? No—not furtive: just careful. They hadn't had a child lying awake in the next room. And the culminating moment, in that bedroom in Spain, had been the epitome of all that was clean and natural.

There had been another thing, which had seemed irrational at the time. When Anne had come home with news that she had got the post in the records office at Scotland Yard, Jean Cossey had been anything but wildly enthusiastic. Later, she had tried to make a weak joke out of it.

'Well—we shall have to look out, shan't we? God knows what you'll be able to find out about some of us.'

A very weak joke indeed. And it wasn't that Anne's mother had ever shown any sympathy with law-breakers. But she had certainly shown no pleasure when Anne had launched herself on that career.

'Are you doing anything special this lunch-time, Anne?'

That was Jane Dewhurst calling across the office.

'Nothing—except avoiding the sight and smell of food.'

'Poor you! Do a swap with me? I need to catch William— and I've only just remembered he's on early turn.'

'Gladly.'

It was a stroke of luck, to be left holding the fort while the others went out. Anne opened every window that would open, rejoiced in the cool draughts, emptied into the waste-paper basket a couple of ashtrays that revolted her. And she took her time over the next few files.

She had always enjoyed lone-wolf duty. This was how she had been working the day she had first met Howard. Shiner had sent him down to try to find some hook-up between one of their cases and something that had happened ages ago. Had it been love at first sight? If not that, at least fascination at first sight—for both of them.

She lifted a file-cover: ELTERSLEY: Allison Elizabeth, Arnos Grove, April 1960.

Then the door opened with a token rap, and Howard came in. And the scene was not exactly as before. She hadn't been glorying in open windows then. Papers hadn't been flutter-ing about on other people's desks. Howard came in and put a sketchy kiss on her cheek.

'I saw Jane in the lift. She said you were standing in for her. Are you fit to be here?'

'I'm as well here as anywhere.'

'It's all very well saying that—'

'It comes and goes, Howard. At the moment it's tolerable.'

'Hadn't you better ask the doctor to give you something?'

'After thalidomide? All I can do is soldier on.'

She tried the right kind of smile, but he did not come back with anything convincing.

'Darling—what have you been saying to my mother?'

Mrs Lawson must have rung him at work. Typical. Didn't she know how men hated that?

'I'm sorry, Howard—but she really did go too far this morning.'

'Mightn't you have misunderstood?'

'Howard—which of us are you going to believe?'

Nausea again—brought on by this, she supposed. But she was objective enough to ask herself whether she was sheltering behind it. She tried to be fair; but sheer physical misery prevailed.

'I don't want to go into all the things that she actually said. It's all so trivial.'

'Trivial it is indeed—little things looming large.'

'I have something large looming inside me at this moment.'

'I know that. And all of us want to do everything for you we can.'

'There's nothing any of you can do until this stage passes.'

'I know that too. But I do want to help. And you must help yourself, too.'

'Is that what your mother says? Well, go on, don't shirk it: what has she sent you to say to me? To pull myself together?'

'Look, Anne—don't get this wrong. Nobody's criticizing. Everybody understands. You've come through a terrible time. But you've got to hold firm—'

'I was under the impression that I was holding firm. I haven't had a miscarriage yet. Is that what your mother wants?'

She knew she was being unreasonable. But it was less trouble than being reasonable—and less answerable.

Howard was lost. It was not the sort of situation he had bargained for—either from marriage or from her. She told herself he was inadequate. He would stay a sergeant all his life. He could not cope. He was inept. This twist in their relationship invited brutal counter-tactics.

'I'm not asking you to choose between us, Howard. It hasn't quite come to that yet.'

'Anne—it's not like you to talk like this. The two women I think most of in the world—and you can't get on together—'

'You'll have to decide which side you're on, won't you?'

'Why should it come to that? It takes two—'

'No—it takes one. I'm not what was hoped for you. That is made plain every time I open my mouth in that house.'

'Only if that's the way you see and hear things.'

'Well, let me tell you this: I don't know how much longer I can take this. I am trying, and I will try. But I can't guarantee myself against the sort of attack that I had to face this morning. And if I don't come home one of these even ings, you'll know it's because I can't face any more of it.'

'Darling—'

'That word is becoming a debased currency.'

The phone rang. She had to take it. It was someone from West Sussex, progress-chasing a report he'd asked Jane for earlier in the day. Anne found the papers on Jane's desk and took a long time reading from them aloud at dictation speed. By the time she had hung up, three of the others were back. Howard could do no more than plant another dry peck on her cheek and make sheepishly for the door.

'See you this evening.'

'I dare say.'

She did not go to eat when she was relieved. She walked down to the Abbey, put her nose into the Dean's Yard, a setting which had had a sedative effect on her before now but which failed to move her today. Her eyes smarted when she thought of the things that she and Howard had said to each other. She was back at her grindstone by three o'clock.

ELTERSLEY: Allison Elizabeth, Arnos Grove, 1960—

It was a story familiar in recent years—a pram-theft from outside a supermarket. The baby had vanished and one of the things that raised hopes of early retrieval had been that it was no ordinary pram. Almost brand new, with prominent springs and high wheels, it could well be unique within a five-mile radius. But it did not show up. Questionnaires produced shoppers who had seen it being pushed both by the mother and the presumed thief. A description of the latter was assembled from a number of sources, and there was convincing agreement: a young woman, certainly not more than twenty, in waist-length nylon fur and light tan plastic boots. That led to interviews with various women—but not to the one that mattered. The media helped. An identical pram was paraded by a policewoman of the right build in the right mufti. Nothing led to the discovery of the Eltersley baby.

So could it have been Jean Cossey who had taken her? And if so, for God's sake why? Insatiable maternal longing after a stillbirth? Jean Cossey had had well-rounded maternal instincts: Anne recognized that now. Had Mr Camel-Leopard been someone who knew about that callous theft? Was it possible—every memory and sentiment in Anne wanted to reject it—that her mother could do so barbarous a thing? And if she had, in some moment of aberration, in which case it was wrong to think in terms of barbarity, what did that make Anne? According to these papers, she'd be the daughter of a man who maintained machinery in a sweet factory. How did Ronald Eltersley compare with Peter Burne Pennyman, Shipping Clerk? It was nevertheless another dossier to bring forward for Kenworthy.

At a quarter past three, Kenworthy went out. They knew that in the general office, because he rang down for them to record a call that he was expecting. A sort of tension was always lifted when Kenworthy left the premises.

Anne turned to her next file. It referred to one of those

fringes of Epping Forest where there were still trees. It was
an Essex case, but there had been massive co-operation from
the Met because the abduction had very probably been into
Greater London.

In 1962, Bernadette Antonia Anselme had apparently
gone up in vapour from the sunny play-garden of a convent-
orphanage. Substitution had played a large part in
Bernadette's life. Her given name had derived from the
saint's day on which she had first been taken into the care of
the sisters. She was a foundling: a carry-cot in a telephone
kiosk. Medical opinion had certified a healthy child, clean
and warmly dressed in new clothes of good quality. Whoever
had abandoned her had not been totally without conscience.
Also in the kiosk had been a couple of dozen new nappies
and a basic kit of safety-pins, cotton wool and patent baby
foods.

Jean Cossey? There was a roundabout concern for
Bernadette's welfare, and that was the way that Anne's
mother had sometimes done things. Had she left the child in
the kiosk, then later, falling on better fortunes, crept in and
taken her back? It posed difficult questions: she would
somehow have had to be able to identify the child and its
whereabouts.

Inquiries into Bernadette's case had led nowhere. Everything possible seemed to have been covered. It would take
any genius Kenworthy possessed to wring anything out of
that file.

Interruption: a call to be recorded for Kenworthy.

'Hold on, please, Superintendent Bartram,' the girl on the
switch-board said. She checked the state of the cassette and
inserted a fresh one. Apparently Bartram had said that he
expected to be talking for a long time.

Another file: Anne lifted the corner of a wad of papers,
thicker than any other she had handled today. The top sheet
was relatively uninformative: a flimsy in which a man called
Toplady informed an officer called Heather that someone

called Guppy had seen these papers and was unhappy about them.

Within a dozen pages, Anne was enthralled. By the twentieth she was conscious of a fluttering change in her pulse rate. Why should she want to be this girl, rather than one of the others? Was it because this sort of origin seemed so much more desirable? More exciting, certainly—

Towards the end of the file, there were a number of envelopes containing exhibits. She sifted through them— then called over to Jane to know whether she had heard Kenworthy come in again yet.

He hadn't. The other girl changed her cassette. Bartram was still at it.

The case on file followed a relatively familiar pattern. Except for one or two features, it was almost a series of criminals' clichés.

A child had been kidnapped, the two-year-old daughter of parents who could have unbuckled a significant ransom. Between these parents, things were not all they might have been. Years of bickering had broken into open warfare. When they saw the ransom conditions they delivered battle on each other afresh. The police had already been informed that the child was missing—had wandered away, it seemed, from a daydreaming nursemaid, from a lawn into a neighbouring woodland. When the demand arrived, the mother let the police know at once. The father thought otherwise. He stormed at his wife. The police would mess about with faked bundles of money, a pick-up point, a timed ambush, insisting that the release of the child should be shrewdly synchronized. It had all happened before. The father did not share the mother's pathetic confidence in the sensitivity of the law. Shrewd synchronization needed sensitive management. One over-conspicuous plain-clothesman, loitering where no man would loiter without purpose, and the whole sequence would be blown. Capital punishment was a thing of the past: they might well kill the child if that was the only way of avoiding a long prison-sentence. It had all happened before.

The parents did not agree to go their own ways. They simply went them. The mother treated with the police, and a Chief Inspector Heather took over the production number. The father knew in outline what was planned. He said that he was happy to see Heather in charge.

In the meanwhile, he himself had contacted the kidnappers, through a channel that they had stipulated. He quite unscrupulously let them know that he was acting independently of his wife, and that if they made any arrangements with her, they would be trapped. They must deliver the child to him, at least twenty-four hours before the curtain time that Heather was proposing. Edwin Booth was apparently that kind of man, that kind of bully.

Edwin Booth—author of a tattered paperback, *Four Marys*, with which Jean Cossey had refused to part for a jumble sale . . .

It was not known to the compiler of the file whether Edwin Booth intended to hand over good money or not. It was not clear whether Chief Inspector Heather knew of his independent plans—or whether Heather was a crafty opportunist, perpetually prepared for everything.

What did happen was that Heather's men were waiting in the wings for Edwin Booth's rendezvous, which took place at a riverside edge of Booth's compact but highly desirable estate. Diane Booth was also out of doors that night, which suggested bad security on somebody's part—another point which the file did not clear up: no wonder Guppy and Toplady had been dissatisfied. There was gunplay under cover of darkness. Diane Booth was shot and died of internal hæmorrhages in hospital at Burford. The child, Edwina, was heard to shout for her parents, and then to scream. There was blood on the grass at a spot close to where her voice had come from. The blood-group was hers.

She was never seen again. Those who had come to collect the ransom—a trio?—a quartet?—made an escape of which

Chief Inspector Heather could not have been proud. His ultimate interview with Toplady and Guppy must have been chillier than anything that went down on paper. Edwina Booth disappeared untraceably, as had Stella Davidge of Northwood Hills, Baby Eltersley of Arnos Grove, and Bernadette Antonia Anselme from the grounds of a nunnery in Epping Forest.

Edwin Booth was a novelist. He had written three runaway bestsellers, one of them a runaway trilogy. He had had two peak-hour television adaptations, which had also done well in the States, and had been sold to more than one European network. He was a man who had anticipated the swinging decade. He had gambled on the outcome of the *Lady Chatterley* trial. His *As Other Men Were* dead-heated with the emancipation of the four-letter word. 'The nineteenth century novel in twentieth century orbit', a reviewer said. 'Balzac on skids. *The Human Comedy* with the brake off.' Some of the less enthusiastic critics were equally pithy. 'Warts *et praetera nihil*,' someone wrote of *Roundhead*.

Diane Booth had been eight years her husband's junior, a *Country Life* frontispiece as Diane Keightley, and heiress to the Ross and Keightley silk mills, where manmade fibres had been anticipated by five patent-registering years. It was his wife's capital that enabled Booth to pull off his most fruitful gamble. He was under no publisher's contract for royalties: he had commissioned his own work on win-all-lose-all terms—he was not a man who ever considered losing. He was, in fact, his own publisher, and did not delegate intermediate stages. For the rest of his creative days, he had gone on pocketing a good deal more than an author's normal share of the takings.

At the time of the kidnapping, his home had been a custom-built villa on the Upper Thames, between Lechlade and Radcot. He was now tax-havened in Jersey.

Anne Lawson had known none of this about him. She had glanced at no more than a page or two of *Four Marys*. It was obvious to her now that she was of exactly the right age to be his daughter. And she liked to think that she had the right sort of mind for the offspring of a creative spirit. It was difficult to see where Jean Cossey could come into the picture, but Kenworthy might have ideas about that.

Anne turned to the packet of photographs, mostly angles of rooms and the grounds of a modern country property: a patio edging a swimming pool. She felt certain that somewhere in the sheaf that she was holding there would be a police technician's shot of the Hobbema avenue. But she riffled through the pictures in vain. There was no such scene: only modern rooms—as modern, at any rate, as the late 1950's—bucket chairs, massive, machine-turned, two-door television consoles, a man's study with a rather ugly microphone to record for an audio-typist.

There were people, too—not posed, not studio portraits, but opportunist shots, taken from long distances by zoom lenses: a transgression against normal police regulations holding on record the activities of people against whom no charge was contemplated. Edwin Booth was amusing himself teaching a pair of Alsatians to jump over a hurdle. His wife was wearing an immaculate gardening apron, pruning a rose. Baby Edwina was crawling by an inlet of river-bank, a setting suitable for Toad, Mole and Water Rat. Anne felt another leap of adrenalin: could that be her at the age of two, in floral dungarees and a frilly sun-bonnet? There was a profile of a girl who must surely be the negligent nursemaid: something familiar about her. Ought Anne to recognize her? An obvious theory erupted, but had to be put down straight away: in no way was this girl like Jean Cossey. Anne carried the portrait over to a better light. There was something supercilious about the girl, who had qualified no doubt on some elite nursery-nursing course, had probably been appointed as much for her social acceptability as for any particular devotion.

There were shots of the child's bedroom: a Beatrix Potter

frieze and a well-ordered line-up of expensive toys, the largest teddy-bear she had ever seen. But there was something else, too—a toy that did not belong to this generation. It was a bird in flight with wings outstretched, a bird made of blue felt, with one eye missing. Even on a print such as this, the gap was visible. And this time Anne knew she was not fantasizing. She knew that bird.

She had always been afraid of it.

CHAPTER 13

'I've said it before, and I'll say it again.'

Bartram's voice breezed from the tape.

'There's nowt so funny as folk.'

However feeble, he had to start with his joke.

'You just can't believe what can be set in motion when Mum and Dad won't extend their tastes in music. Neither would young Jean.'

'There's been murder for less,' Kenworthy muttered to himself. 'Stone the crows, Bartram—get on with it.'

'Black and White Minstrel Show, that was about the measure of Ma and Pa Pogson's musicology. Note the name: Pogson. I don't know where she dug the Cresswell and the Carter and the Cossey from. Anyway, she was a right little rock'n' roller when she was fourteen. Bill Haley, Chubby Checker, Enis the Penis. Of course, this was before the Beatles. I've said it before, and I'll say it again—'

When the blazes was he going to come to the point?

'What was I on about? They used to call some of us squares. The Pogsons were so square, they could have shat potato-chips. They were the first generation everything. First generation to have more than ninepence credit at the corner shop. First generation to be able to put ten per cent down on their own house.

'But that's progress, you see, Kenworthy—and there's nowt so deadly as progress. Progress makes people respectable—and that can be a right killer. Ernie Pogson's father had been out of work right through the 'thirties. Spent all of every morning dubbining Ernie's football boots—just to have something to do. Supplest bit of football leather on Lower Shitheap Recreation Ground, Ernie had on his feet. Then the war took Ernie places: Padgate, RAF armourer. Went up in the world, if not in an aeroplane. Leading aircraftman: got a propeller on his arm by the time he was demobbed. Bizerta. Cairo. Saw the Great Pyramid. Came home and found his mother had taken up cigarette-smoking at the age of eighty-three. Don't worry, Kenworthy—I'm coming to it.

'Ernie's demobbed. Gets taken on at Potter's. Office job. Marries Liz Beadle, white wedding, topped off with ham salad at Robinson's caff. Liz Beadle had grown up arse-rag poor up Snothole Nab: that's Lancashire for Stonehill Bank. The most respectable crap-pile in the County Palatine, is Snothole. More chapels than pubs. No cross, no crown, you know. People have to have something to believe in, even up Snothole.

'Enter Jean. First generation Pogson or Beadle to go to a grammar school. Won the scholarship, as they still called it. Big future for her: brilliant woman surgeon, first female barrister with chambers in Toe-Rag Street. Matron of Bloodbottle Hospital. Well—she might have made it into a bank or a library, but that wasn't what she wanted. Musical: Johnny Mathis and Cliff Richard. When she was fifteen, she put her name down for a crooning competition at the Phoenix Hotel. Old Ernie went spare. I feel for him, poor old sod.

'She'd all these records of the Everley Brothers, Guy Mitchell, Freddy Fart-Arse and his Fanny-fumbling Five. Life in that house was one livelong bloody battle—and it was all about music. Of course they'd bought her a record-player.

Of course they were delighted when her friends came round, jealous of it. But once their munificence had been put on show, it lost its purpose as far as Ma and Pa were concerned. And what was the use of a record-player when they were always wanting it off because Friday Night was Music Night?

'Then Gwen Beecham went to live in London. That was what did it. Gwen Beecham has a lot to answer for. She was a year or two older than Jean. She used to see her across the road when Jean was a Mixed Infant. I got most of what I'm telling you from Gwen Beecham. If you remember, old Nellie Gregory wasn't impressed by Gwen. Well, that's less than fair, because I don't see much wrong with her, except what life's dealt her. But she was one of those who wanted away from the cotton valleys—and she was one of the first of her lot to make it. And there was nothing unrespectable about her early London days—except for a tendency to talk a bit larger than life. She went to London, started off living with her mother's cousin, did a run-of-the-mill commercial course, sighed for independence, and went to live at the YWCA. And she surely did get around: she could even afford a pop concert once a month. She got the autograph of a man called Johnny Pewter—even reckons to have spoken to him. That was big stuff to write to young Jean about. Why don't you come to London when you leave school? No place like it.

'You and I know, Kenworthy—you a lot better than me—how many kids did that. We've lost a tidy lot from up here. You know how many you picked up and sent home—and you've some notion of how many you didn't. And Jean hadn't been there long before she became an embarrassment to Gwen Beecham. Gwen had never believed the kid would actually show up, just like that, with no job, no training, and so-called savings that wouldn't pay more than a week or two's rent. And Jean must have seen through Gwen in a day or two. Where the hell was Johnny Pewter? Gwen took her to see him from the back of the upper circle; she could have managed that at the Manchester Palace. And Gwen was a working girl. She came home hungry and tired of an evening. Jean had time on her hands. She started finding her own friends, one in particular, a lass who called herself Angela. Gwen took an active dislike to that one.'

And it was at this point in the tape that one of the most glacial and self-glorious of the top corridor secretaries rang. Would Chief Superintendent Kenworthy report to the Commander at seven minutes past eleven, please? That was one of the Commander's gimmicks—settling the brevity of appointments in advance.

'Yes,' Kenworthy said. 'I'll be there. What does he think he is—a blooming train?'

Anne read the Booth file again slowly, checking each personality in turn against the photographs. Could she really have lived in that house, in those grounds? Could she have played along that stretch of river-bank? Was she in danger of forcing false memories on herself? She studied the pictures of Mrs Booth, tried to imagine what it would be like, having a woman like that for a mother: a woman in her thirties, who did not have to do mental arithmetic in supermarkets, who complained when she wasn't properly noticed by the *Tatler*; who didn't keep her gin in a walnut wardrobe. There was something extraordinarily new about the gardening apron, as if she had put it on only for that moment, and would never wear it again. Anne could not imagine calling her *Mummy*.

Yet the memory of the hanging bluebird was indelible. She had always hated that bird. She had been afraid of it, as one is afraid of the unnatural and unnamed. It had once scorched its way into the sick dreams of a childhood fever. It smelled of dust and departed generations. She remembered screaming for it to be taken away. And they had taken it away, though not out of the room. They had hung it over in a far corner, and she was afraid of turning over in bed, for fear she should see it.

Anne stayed in the office after the others had gone, telling them she was making up the time she had lost this morning. She waited until it was too late for any of the commuter trains at which she usually aimed. At half past six she wrote a covering note to Kenworthy and took the files up to his room. The cleaners were already in. She put the folders down conspicuously on his desk. One of his pipes lay in its bowl of ash, its bowl unevenly charred, the mouthpiece dented by his corner teeth.

As she checked herself out at the front desk, she was beginning to feel light-headed: she had eaten no food all day. She told herself that she had enough common sense to try to eat something before committing herself to British Rail. She had always found the surrounds of Victoria disappointing snack country, but there was one stand-up counter that she had found tolerable in the past. She ordered a cheese sandwich. And tea or coffee? The thought of either was repellent. There was alleged orangeade in a container that had two plastic fruit floating round in it. She asked for a glass and, oddly, it seemed to be what her system was craving. But after two bites at the sandwich, she laid it aside.

She looked at her watch, was happy to see that she had missed yet another train. They would be growing uneasy at the Lawsons' now. What would happen if she were to live up to her half-threat and not go 'home'? Why shouldn't she put up at a hotel somewhere? She knew in the centre of her brain that she would do no such thing. But it was amusing—and comforting—to pretend that she had not made up her mind about it yet. At this rate, it would be getting on for nine before she was home, anyway. And when she did get there, she'd go straight to bed. Horizontality was what her condition demanded. She thought of the microscopic little fish-like creature that Howard had activated inside her. When were she and Howard going to get the chance to be themselves?

Outside the café buses were edging forward like great red bullies, nosing into the flocks of street-crossers. The peak-hour tide was spent, but hordes were still charging both ways, as if every man, woman and child were under some nightmare urge to be on the move. She leaped out of the way of a taxi, did not catch what was said by the driver of another one that she had not seen. Every telephone-box under the entrance arch was occupied. That was a good excuse for not making the call that she had no intention of making, anyway. Let them wonder.

A man stepped forward from among the loose scrum outside the kiosks, holding out a 50p piece.

'Do you happen to have change?'

He would be in his early forties, might once have been considered good-looking—by some. Certainly he had not yet given up fancying himself. She was tempted to show him the sight of her shoulders, told herself not to be churlish, stopped to look in her bag, though she felt certain she was not carrying so much coin. He thanked her, and made a rush for a kiosk that someone was leaving.

She went and found an empty compartment: one recompense at least for working late. The floor was filthy, the windows grimed, obscenities pointlessly scrawled on the walls. Heads and shoulders passed the window, eyes looked in at her, passed on. Then the door opened, men were rushing in past her knees, a lot of them, it seemed, and noisy, conscious only of their own entity, as if they were a rugger team on the move. They had been drinking, were laughing loudly at something recently shared. Somebody clambered clumsily over her feet, someone else sat down at her side, not looking what he was doing, setting his buttocks down on an open flap of her coat. She tried to tug it away from him.

'I'm sorry,' he said, got up to release her, looking at her with sexy appraisal, breathing beer into her face. She pressed herself impossibly tighter into the window-corner. The man was leaning against her heavily now, trying to get at something in his pocket: cigarettes, though it was a non-smoker. Something hurt her arm. He continued to lean.

'Excuse me.'

She made signs that she wanted to stand up. He got up himself to allow her to do so. She opened the door, got out, walked down the train, found a compartment with only one or two in it. Ten minutes after the time-tabled departure time, she was still staring at the same patch of grey platform.

Sleep of a sort settled over her as they hauled up to Battersea: dreams that weren't dreams—images that merged—the child by the river's edge—the arrogant nurse-maid. Brixton. Clapham. Herne Hill. Her eyes opened, saw a blue signboard over an office in a siding: *Approved Coal Merchant*. Her eyes closed again, saw Diane Booth's rose-pruning apron. Worn to be photographed pruning that one bush?

In an instantaneous lifting of her eyelids, she glimpsed the playing fields of Dulwich College, the green fading into twilight. Then a deeper sleep engulfed her, no mere head-nodding cat-nap. She sank down into an immeasurable gulf of dreamlessness. She felt as if she were both in sleep and out of it, seeing her own sleep from outside it. It was like being in hospital: anæsthetics. She had had her appendix out when she was twelve, had felt the pain and the apprehension fade away under pre-medication. Then had come the tiniest prick in the back of her hand: not painful, not even startling. Paradoxically, it had been gratifying, an assurance that someone was caring for her, that the anæsthetist was her friend.

Timelessness. She was no longer outside her sleep. In the hospital that time, when it was all over, she had wakened first momentarily, to see the square lines of the ward window opposite, a carafe of water, a *Get Well* card on her locker.

But now she was coming to in a jolting, tobacco-ridden chilliness, a gut-heaving stale dustiness of car upholstery. She was on the back seat. A man and a woman were in front of her. She closed her eyes again. But then she forced herself jerkily awake, grasping for understanding.

She was in a car, sprawled out on the seat. Over the heads of the couple in front of her, she could see the unkempt hedges of a neglected lane. And trees: Hobbema's trees. No: they were not Hobbema's trees. They were different from Hobbema's. But these were *the* trees.

My God—

CHAPTER 14

The fulcrum of the Lawsons' evening was to have been the thirteenth and final instalment of *Is he Popenjoy?* after the nine o'clock news. But none of them could concentrate. When Howard's father got up and switched off the set after five or six minutes of the play, that was the feeling of the meeting.

Not that it was late enough yet for them to have quite run out of rational explanations. The one thing that neither Howard nor his mother had mentioned was Anne's veiled threat to find somewhere else to live. At half past eight, Howard had rung up the Yard, but Anne's department was shut down for the night. He rang Jane Dewhurst at home. All she could tell him was that Anne had said she would work late. It was easy to picture her taken ill on the way home. She ought not to have been at her desk at all today. It was not feasible for one man to ring every casualty department to which she might have been taken between SW1 and these south-eastern extremities, but Howard started making a list of the major ones. At a few minutes after ten, he rang Wright's home. Shiner was out, but his wife was an affable woman to whom he found it somehow easier to explain the situation than it would have been to Shiner.

'I'll tell him as soon as he comes in. I'm sure everything will come out in the wash. Do let me know if you hear any news in the meanwhile.'

Just after half past eleven, Shiner rang back himself.

'You've got on to the hospitals?'

'All the big ones.'

'Try British Rail. They probably have no machinery for collating minor incidents, but if anything out of the ordinary has happened, someone may know about it.'

Nothing. But it was customary for the arches and concourse of Victoria Station to be manned by an unobtrusive detective-constable, and the one on duty knew Anne by sight, having met her at some social function. He had seen her come through the main entrance, had watched her open her bag and look for change for the man outside the telephones. Then he had moved over to keep an eye on a beery bunch who were converging on the Sevenoaks train. He saw Anne come out of their compartment and find herself another. He did not blame her for that.

But it was not until fairly late the next morning that this piece of information was paid into the system: the officer concerned had gone off duty, and did not learn until mid-morning what had happened to Anne. Inquiries were by that time strung out over a distance, and everything was being gone into, however unlikely it seemed. Thus another memorandum that reached Wright's desk at about the same time was that last night a woman had been taken off Shortlands Station, between Beckenham and Bromely, in a wheel-chair—a folding model that had been carried in the guard's van. There was nothing to connect her with Anne. No description worth having. But the item was logged: a woman travelling with companions—a man and a woman.

Hobbema's trees—

Anne had no idea what time of day it was. Actually, it was very early morning, with dewy dampness in ill-kempt hedgerows, a good deal of busy bird-life—and no signs of human activity. It was that kind of lane which in the Fen country is called a Drove—a straight and unmetalled road, overgrown with grasses, that led between the drainage channels of the low-lying land.

But Anne did not take the landscape in immediately. Despite the need to be alert, her desire for sleep was still uppermost. But the wheels were bumping cruelly along the earthy ruts, which did not make for comfort. She tried to do something about her position. Her head was twisted backwards and her neck felt as if it were breaking. The circulation in her right arm seemed to have stopped.

This was not the Hobbema dream. This avenue was for real. There were bulrushes growing at the edge of a dyke: they were real bulrushes. The water in the ditch was floating with green weed. A coot retreated frantically as they passed. About the tangled vegetation, even about the light of the barely developed dawn, there was a reality, a chilly commonplaceness too convincing for dream.

So where was she? Holland? Flanders? She was not sure of the nationality of Old Master Hobbema. But she had rejected Hobbema, hadn't she? Her mind did not seem to be working in logical steps: was jumping about irrationally from one plane to another. She could see the landscape stretching out in unrelieved flatness to the horizon on all quarters. And, exactly as in the dream, there was the vital divergence from Hobbema: the trees led her eye up to a house. It was an ancient house, timber and plaster, the eighteenth century imposed on the seventeenth, evolved from the sixteenth and fifteenth, probably on much earlier foundations.

'I'm going to be sick.'

The woman in the front passenger seat turned and looked over her shoulder. It was Angela, Jean Cossey's most recent friend, suave as ever in intention, with a certain shining greasiness under her eye-sockets, as if a long night was beginning to be too much for her too. And as the man at the wheel also turned, Anne saw from his profile that he was someone that she had been before. But she could not yet place him in her mind.

'We shall be there in a minute,' Angela said. 'Hold on if
you can.'

But Anne was not able to oblige. She heaved and retched.
Angela told the driver to stop, got out and came to the door,
helped her out ot the edge of the ditch. There was a cold bite
in the morning. Anne tried to be sick again, failed, and did
not see how she was going to remain on her legs.

'Do you think you can walk to the house?'

It was about seventy yards away.

'I know I can't. I feel awful.'

'You'll feel better in a little while, once you get indoors,
and into a bed, and with something warm inside you.'

Angela was not being particularly sympathetic: simply
practical.

'Where is this place? Where are we? What is happening?'

The man looked at her with unconcealed hostility, assess-
ing her as of sexual habit, rejecting her because of her present
state of wretchedness. He needed a shave. He must have
been driving most of the night.

Anne tried to walk a step, tottered groggily, supported
herself against the open car door. She looked at the man
again and was able to place the face she had seen under the
arches at Victoria, asking her for change for the phone. But
then the certainty vanished from her again. She could not
think. Nothing made sense.

'All right. Get back in the car.'

They reached the house without getting up speed.

Kenworthy had taken to arriving at his office early. It helped
him to bear BR(SR) at its worst: he did not bring his car into
SW1 these days.

He had got into the habit of walking round the office before
anyone arrived. He did not interfere with anything—
but information, he told himself shamelessly, was always
where you could get it: somebody's in-tray that did not
look as if anything had shifted in it since the day before yes-

terday. And how far on its rounds had his last *All to see* memo gone?

There was little to note this morning—except that Anne Lawson's desk was clear. He went upstairs. The morning mail—even the overnight internal—had not yet arrived. The cassette of Bartram's tape was lying tidily on top of the files that Anne had laid there. He set it aside, picked up the first of what Anne had brought him.

She was a good lass—one of the few in the office who had really grasped the sort of thing that they were looking for. Pity she couldn't stand pipe smoke.

He was not impressed by the unsolved stealing from a pram, almost a quarter of a century ago: hardly the depth of field he'd have looked for in Jean Cossey. Unless, of course, this had been an aberration—and she had spent the rest of her life trying to live up to the worst mistake she'd ever made. Wasn't that roughly what he thought she'd been doing, anyway? Maybe: but it had to have been something a bit less casual than a pram outside a supermarket. That wouldn't have led her to a path-crossing course with Swannee Foster; at least, Kenworthy could not at this moment see how.

Abduction from a nunnery garden? That must surely have been some family affair—Catholics, Irish, all that. How the hell did an imbecilic crime like that manage to go unsolved? It made Kenworthy think that somebody hadn't been bloody well trying.

He thought back to Stella Davidge. It was on the cards that Stella Davidge had become Jean Cossey; yet somehow the notion did not appeal to him. There was something about Jean Cossey that leaped at him from between her lines. He believed that there had been an earthiness about her, a quick wit, ready to grab the opportunities of the moment; a resolution not to be put down by frustrations. Slodden-le-Woods had been rotten for that pair; but it had been the escape that Jean Cossey had seen for them, and she had stuck it out. That was not a spirit that one naturally associated with the bowler-hat belt. That sort of staying-power was usually the product of a sub-tribal moulding. To build up that core of intuition, you needed hardship behind you. Stella Davidge and Jean Cossey would not have gone for the same sort of man. Stella would have gone for someone who talked riding-school language—another from along the Marylebone line—or else someone who had dropped out of that ethos because he found it as repugnant as she did. It was possible to think of Stella Davidge besotted by an anarchist. But could you imagine Jean Cossey listening to politics—or even anti-politics—for more than twenty minutes or so?

Kenworthy opened the thick file. And the very first memo-slip brought him to life: Toplady, Guppy, Heather—those were names to juggle with, if you still sighed occasionally for the days before the rot set in. Guppy had been an Assistant Commissioner (Crime) whom you kept out of the way of—unless you were winning. Toplady had been Detective Chief Superintendent before they had started throwing the rank of Commander about as lavishly as they did these days. And if it had been Sid Heather's case, and he had not closed it, then it must have been a rough business.

The first time through, Kenworthy did not read every page. He got hold of the gist without that—but he did not propose to wait long before getting down to the detail. He rang down to see if Anne had arrived yet. The first flutter of the day was just beginning. Shiner was trying to get through to him on one line, the Commander on another.

'Anne Lawson didn't get home last night.'

'Kenworthy—what have you got on dead files about missing children, nineteen-fifty-eight to 'sixty-one? Let me have abstracts as soon as you can of all those that went unaccounted for. And don't forget what I told you yester-day.'

Yesterday, at 11.07, Commander Cawthorne had been in that mood where he got things done by shafts of unbarbed.

irony; the barbs came later, if he hadn't proved his point in the preliminary knock-up.

'Looks to me as if you have more than a finger in this pie that DI Wright is cooking up, Kenworthy.'

'He did come over and talk a few things over with me. We had something in the annals.'

'Which helps to show why our computerizing is fifteen per cent behind target.'

'That target was tentative, if you remember. We'd no real idea then how much reading there was going to be.'

'I just want you to know that I'm taking personal charge of this case, Kenworthy. I'm not averse to help from any man. But I need to have it clear in my mind what help I'm getting—in advance.'

'Sir.'

Kenworthy never saw any harm in verbal agreement. It saved vexatious arguments. And if there was a Commander for whom he did not give a bugger, it was Cawthorne.

CHAPTER 15

They hustled her in. She formed impressions, but was not allowed to let her eye rest too inquisitively on things. She was aware of a glow of old furniture, a warming-pan, low ceilings, old brown beams, angles listing from subsidence.

They pushed her upstairs to a mercifully quiet and airy room that was clearly on the least frequented flank of the house. It overlooked a neglected orchard: trees with twisted inner boughs that had not been pruned for years: bindweed taking over gooseberry bushes.

The couple left her immediately. She heard the key in the lock. The window had close-set horizontal bars. It was a room custom-adapted as a prison. She must have been here before—but how and when? She knew now that the

Hobbema dream was a thrown-up remnant of memory. But what set of circumstances . . . ?

She could not think. She gave up trying to think. She laid herself fully clothed on the bed and let her eyes close. It could have been half an hour, it could have been three hours, when she was wakened by someone opening her door. It was Angela, apparently rested, her make-up renewed.

'Hi!'

Spontaneous enough. Anything but unfriendly.

'Still feeling bloody? Just a touch of anæsthetic. I'm sorry we had to put you out. You'll take no harm.'

'I'm not so sure. I'm pregnant. I ought to see a doctor.'

'Pregnant, are you? I didn't think anyone ever had honeymoon babies these days. You're just the sort who'd let that happen to you, aren't you?'

Derisive; but not with the cutting edge of embittered hostility.

'How far are you?'

'A few weeks.'

'Yes, well, we'll keep an eye on you. We need you in good fettle. As for a doctor—you'll be seeing your own in a day or two, I hope.'

'Would you mind telling me—?'

'Everything—in due course. We shan't get far unless we have you with us—wholeheartedly. But something to eat, first—'

'It'll have to be something pretty neutral.'

'Cereal? Toast, drop of milk? Tea? Coffee?'

'Tea, please. Weak. China, if possible. And I want to know—'

'China's doubtful, but I'll look and see. And don't break your head with questions. I've already said—you need to be sound in mind and body. We'll pull you round. And you've nothing to worry about. Far from it. This is all for your own good.'

'How long are you going to keep me here?'

'Two or three days. I hope it won't be longer. It depends
on one or two things we can't control.'

'Who's *we*? You and that horrible man in the car?'

Angela permitted herself a thin smile.

'Len? You find him a little unrefined, do you? And not
exactly the Brain of Britain? I'll admit he'd probably never
have made detective-sergeant. Not with the exams they
make them take these days.'

'I wish you'd tell me—'

'Later. Relax. You're among friends.'

'It's a new kind of friendship to me.'

'You've led too sheltered a life. Go and freshen yourself up
a bit. There's a washbasin in the alcove. You'll have to let me
take you to the lav for the time being. I'll be back in a few
minutes with a tray. Then I suggest more sleep. If there's
anything within reason that you want, there's no harm in
asking. You'll be back with your husband and friends within
a day or two—a good deal better off than you are now.'

There was a hard edge to Angela's cheerfulness. It was a
cheerfulness that Anne did not find infectious. But there
seemed to be something in the suggestion that she was not
going to be badly looked after. On the rack above the
washbasin they had provided her with a choice of soaps,
toothpaste, a new brush, dental floss, toilet water.

The hot weak tea did her good. The toast gave her
digestion something to work on. The sleep came, real sleep,
in clean new sheets and a new nightdress provided by
Angela. Whatever questions were unanswerable, whatever
cudgelled her brain, it was sleep that had to win. When she
woke up again, she knew that a day was almost over. The
light over the orchard was failing.

'Aye, well, Jean and Gwen grew, as you might say, apart.
Gwen had spotted the sort of company that Jean and Angela
were keeping. She'd tried a brief, sisterly chat—just once. I
think Gwen was probably a little bit high-minded in those

days, when she heard duty calling. But after the reception she got for her preaching, she didn't have a second try. Jean drifted off into her own orbit—or Angela's. Gwen said she felt guilty about it. But I told her—what had she to be guilty about? A nice lass, Kenworthy. Pity her own marriage has gone down the plughole.

'They didn't part enemies, just edged out of each other's circle, though they went on exchanging letters every other Christmas. Until Slodden. Gwen had settled up there—married a lad she'd known at school. Then Jean suddenly telephoned her from Broadstairs.

'Big trouble—but Gwen never got to know what it was really about. There were odd moments when Jean looked as if she was on the verge of the confessional—but she always pulled herself back. She was beside herself, something had gone radically wrong in her life. Gwen must find her a job, must find her digs, must find her a babysitter. She had to lose herself. Where better than working for a living in a place where no woman would be if she didn't have to work there for a living?

'They didn't see a lot of each other in Slodden, Jean and Gwen. Gwen had her own life. She tried to be hospitable. Jean was a loner. But there was one thing, Gwen told me, that she had to give her: she looked after her child. She couldn't dress her too well on her Slodden pay-packet, but she kept her scrupulously clean. And she taught her manners. Half a minute—my lass has just brought me a coffee.'

There was a clicking on and off of the recording switch, then Bartram had deliberately recorded himself slurping at his cup.

'Then it was suddenly ta-ta, Slodden. Slodden over and out. So it's over to you, too, Kenworthy. It was your patch she moved down to.'

'Roger,' Kenworthy said to himself.

★

Someone had visited the room while Anne had been asleep.
There was a tray of sandwiches on the table by the window, a
bottle of Perrier. The parallel with the Spanish hotel was
poignant. She drank half a glass, felt better for it, went into
the alcove and sluiced her face. She had not been at the basin
more than a few seconds when she heard the lock of her door.
They must be keeping close tabs on her. Perhaps her room
was bugged. Or maybe they could tell from the plumbing.
Angela came in briskly.

'Rested? You've slept all day. Anything you want, you can
at least try me. I can't manage miracles, but you might be
surprised at what I can rustle up.'

Nothing could have sounded more genuinely companion-
able. But then, startlingly, she came close behind Anne,
pulled at her nightdress behind the shoulder.

'Hey! What are you doing?'

'Just looking. It's fainter than I'd hoped, but it's there,
right enough.'

They were facing each other now. There was more than a
hint of amused cruelty in Angela's eyes.

'You may not believe this—but I used to hate you. Do you
remember anything at all of those days? When you were
Edwina Booth?'

'Why don't you stop playing with me? Tell me what it's
about. I know I've been here before.'

'Too true you have!'

Anne's brain leaped a stage.

'You were the nursemaid.'

Angela had changed a good deal since the photograph
annexed to the file. But now she was across the gap. Anne
could believe in the resemblance.

'You know, you're smarter than you sometimes have me
thinking,' Angela said. 'Nursemaid? Yes—that was one way
of earning a living. Well—let's say it had its perks.'

She laughed—not a nice laugh.

'Anyway, thank God my duties weren't limited to you. If

you don't mind a spot of bluntness, I thought you were a horrible little brat. But we got by, by and large, you and I. As I hope we're going to get by again now. I'm sure we shall—if we both make allowances. I promise you, I'll do my best on my side.'

Anne looked round for a towel. Angela handed it to her.

'And don't ask too many questions, young lady. How many times did you hear me say that when you were Edwina?'

Anne went back and sat on the bed.

'Still feeling sorry for yourself? You've no need to. If ever a girl had it made—'

'So you keep hinting. How would you like to be in my position, not knowing?'

'Well, I'll tell you. You've got to know. It might make you an easier patient to nurse.'

Angela went idly to the window, looked vacantly out at the ancient apple-trees.

'You were kidnapped. I dare say you've worked that out by now. And now you're going back. You're going back where you came from. You're going to be in the money. And you won't be the only one. There'll be commission in it for one or two others.'

A blackbird flew across the skyline.

'You were kidnapped, and your father—Edwin Booth—had his own way of playing it. Remember him? The big man. He got ahead of his wife and the police—but only to let it be known that they could whistle for their ransom. He didn't want you back—any more than he wanted to keep your mother. They had finished together—all bar the paperwork. And what would he want with you? That was a right turn-up for an abduction squad, wasn't it? They'd done him a favour. A one and a half times millionaire—that's all he was in those days: and he didn't give a pinch of shit for you, my love. You were an embarrassment to him. He had other places to go. When his wife was killed in the shoot-out, that was more than he'd ever dared have prayed for. What would he have had to pay her in maintenance? And you're lucky to be alive, kiddo.'

Anne looked at her, bewildered by the mixture: a voice for all situations, including compassion—and behind it the suggestion of ruthlessness without limit.

'You were lucky. Jean Cossey rescued you, the sentimental little fool.'

Anne's expression made her laugh.

'So can't you work it out that no harm can come to you? To be of any use to us, you've got to be hale and well. You're going back to your father. He's on his way back to the mainland right now. And I repeat, my spoiled little pet, you're in clover for the rest of your days. You'll go back to your detective-sergeant with a bank account you can do things with. You can have your baby, and half a dozen others—and we'll all live happy ever after.'

She went over and turned on the television set, which Anne had noticed for the first time in a corner: a black and white portable. They were in mid-item of the news, some trouble at the Perkins-Diesel factory in Peterborough. Then came a close-up of Anne, blown-up from one of her wedding photographs.

Angela laughed.

CHAPTER 16

Kenworthy knew that Swannee Foster was the key man. But Swannee was the sort of live wire you didn't fiddle with till you made sure you were properly earthed. So he went to see Sid Heather first.

Sid had eight borrowed years already behind him, and their physical effect was pathetic: they showed what all men must come to. But he was mentally alert, had not stopped reading since the moment of his retirement. Sometimes he had to rummage in his brain for a name—but he always found it eventually.

Sid had never made headlines. He had never had a sensational case. But all his cases had been crimes. Heather was a DIs' DI. During most of the years that Kenworthy's time had overlapped with his, Heather had been on an inside job, Chief Inspector, specializing in cross-references and co-ordination for officers out in the field. No one had ever heard what Sid thought about sitting at a desk. He had never said. He had accepted the change—and got on with his assignment. Kenworthy had been glad of his services more than once. And today Heather was glad to see Kenworthy.

'Edwin Booth, writer—Diane Booth, wife thereof, shot dead in post-kidnapping affray—Edwina Booth, infant, blood shed on the grass in the same incident. Otherwise vanished without trace. What can you tell me, Sid?'

'Len Basset,' Sid said.

'I don't think I know the gentleman.'

'I dare say you wouldn't. Small fry. Yet for small fry, he was now and then on the perimeter of big things. Nowadays he'd be called a special contract man: he had control, more or less, of a small but vicious heavy mob. The term special contract hadn't come in at the time of the Booth case. And he wasn't under contract, anyway. He was working for himself.'

'I don't remember seeing his name on the file,' Kenworthy said.

'Because I never did believe in committing guesswork to paper: though this wasn't guesswork. I had Bassett's name as a tip-off. I believed that tip-off—and I believe it still. But Bassett went down for a silly, scruffy little job that gave him a perfect alibi for the Booth kidnapping: it happened at the same time. It was bottom of the league stuff—a village post-office, a hundred quid in notes, a sheet or two of insurance stamps and the Barnardo box. This was in Houghton-le-Spring. County Durham, a long way from the Thames Valley: nylon stocking and Balaclava helmet. His

defence was pathetic, but he only got a short sentence, a few
months. It was a nasty business, the whole thing. There was
something rotten about everybody connected with that case.
I never did believe that Booth cared a bugger whether he got
the kid back or not. All that mattered to him was showing us
that he was half a trick smarter than we were. Oh, he said all
the expected things, threw the right rages, drank all the extra
doubles and more. He might have been acting out a scenario
for one of his own books. Simon—if I tell you where I keep
my Scotch, can I trust you not to be mean with it?'

Kenworthy poured them both stiff measures.

'So you weren't able to take the Durham job to pieces?'

'They wouldn't believe me,' Heather said.

'Who were they?'

'Toplady and Guppy.'

'I always thought they lived on Olympus.'

'They did. With *No Trespassing* notices. They were a couple
of right buggers to work for. But I can see their point now,
even if I did feel sore about it at the time. I had no
evidence—and they knew I was going to get none.'

'It does look a bit thin, Sid—with this Bassett spilling his
marbles in Houghton-le-Spring.'

'I'd had this tip-off. A one hundred per center. I'd have
been ready to stake my wardrobe on it. But he was a difficult
grass. He had a thing about grassing—a bigger thing than
most. He was a sort of grass inside a grass. He'd never have
gone into the box: he'd never have been *let* inside the box. He
wouldn't speak plainly, even though he badly wanted to sink
Basset. He seemed to think that once I knew Basset's name,
that was all I needed. He blamed *me* for not chucking Basset
straight in the slammer.'

'Dare I ask? You're out of it now, Sid—'

These things were dyed in the fleece. An informant's
identity was sacrosanct. Even mountain-bound immortals
were supposed not to ask. Did Sid intend to carry his
prerogative with him into the frontier wilderness of senility?

'Swannee Foster,' Sid said.

'That's not the first time his name's come up. I keep meaning to go and see him. I haven't got round to it yet. Got to give Lionel Friedman the chance to clear his patch first. You see, Sid, we now feel pretty certain the Booth kid survived. She had a foster-mother, recently electrocuted in her bath.'

'I know. I've read about it.'

'But I don't see the connection between Jean Cossey and Edwina Booth. Do you?'

There was something sphinx-like about Sid Heather. And he was not above a bit of presentation, a bonus of play-acting, even at this stage. Kenworthy let it go: he'd get at it some other way.

'They ought never to have retired you, Sid. But let me go on. This foster-mother thing is a bit of a riddle. The woman herself was a riddle. Sometimes she seems to have been as naive as they come—and yet she did have her brighter moments. What I can't make out, is what was she doing in the Booth business in the first instance?'

'Child-minding, I would think,' Heather said. 'After the child was taken, and until she was delivered back. I suppose she developed her own relationship with the kid.'

'So she must have been rubbing shoulders with some of the top people involved. And with top people who might not have been involved. Like Swannee Foster. Because when it was duff birth certificates she wanted, she knew to go to Swannee for them. And Lionel Friedman—he told me to go to Swannee, too.'

'Then maybe it's time you did. Give him my kind regards when you do. And I wouldn't leave it too long. That young lady is distinctly expendable—whether she's really Edwina Booth or not.'

'It isn't even my case, Sid. I've been told very nicely, very obliquely, not to interfere: bags of side-spin—barely kissed the ivory. But the Commander wants the glory of this one.'

'Which Commander?'

'Do I need to tell you? Cawthorne. Don't get me on to that subject. It's some time since I travelled by air. I'm low on vomit bags.'

Sid Heather looked at him with quizzical accusation.

'If you ask me, Simon—which I'm sure you don't—you've wasted too many of your years resenting Cawthorne.'

'All the same—'

'You'll find no tie-up between Swannee and Cawthorne.'

'That's more than I could hope for.'

'Yes, well—don't let me lead you astray, Simon.'

Kenworthy wondered for a long time what old Sid meant by that. He even decided that at Sid's age, it might mean nothing at all.

CHAPTER 17

'Relax, for God's sake,' Angela said. 'I've told you the form.'

'I've been in more relaxing situations.'

'Then let this one be relaxing. Hasn't it sunk in to you yet what this is worth to you? You'll be lying awake at night wondering how you're going to spend it all. And you're not breaking any laws. Be yourself. Prove you're yourself: that's what we've got to start working on now. Damn it, if he were my father, I'd be dying to get in on the act.'

'It seems to me you are in on it.'

The door opened without a knock and the man came in—the man from Victoria Station. He had a Minolta round his neck, set up with a flash unit.

'OK, show me,' he said to Angela, virtually ignoring Anne.

'Come over here, Anne. Where do you want her, Len? Under the window? Take your blouse off.'

'I say, she's not all that badly put together, is she?'

'Take your eyes off her. She's up the spout.'

Basset walked slowly round her.

'That's when they're at their most loving, first three months with one in the pod. That's when they really want it—isn't it, darling? Never mind, my old love. A couple of hours with your old Dad, and you'll be getting it legal and general again. Fancy being shagged by a London copper!'

Every top instinct was to rebel, to refuse to play their game. But Anne also saw other things with a once-in-a-lifetime clarity. If she appeared to obstruct these two, she was likely to get hurt; and she was doubly vulnerable. If Angela felt obliged to turn off her tactical sweetness, something pretty nasty was likely to come in its place.

The man Len moved behind her, focusing.

'It looks bloody faint to me,' he said. 'Booth's going to need more than this. Why the hell couldn't you have warts, or six toes, you bloody moron?'

'She'll start remembering soon,' Angela said.

Len took several shots, and then—more than Anne had hoped for—left the room.

'There are times when Len isn't exactly the ideal district visitor,' Angela said. 'It isn't his bed-*side* manner that he's ever cultivated.'

'Are you chained to him for life, then?'

'He gets better when you get to know him. He was very generous to Jean Cossey. Otherwise you'd have had a thin time. Eighteen years! A bloody lifetime!'

Eighteen years: a familiar term—and one that brought fresh enlightenment to Anne.

'I think I know who you are,' she said.

'Know who I am? What the hell do you mean? Well: I hope it brings you some satisfaction. Go on, tell me: who am I?'

'Swap!' Anne said.

'Swap? What do you mean, swap?'

'Tell me about my mother.'

'Your mother? What is there to tell? Cossetted. Spoiled.
Over-sexed. Over-bedded, at one period. But dear Edwin
had got over that.'

'I don't mean the Booths. I mean the woman who brought
me up: Jean.'

'Stupid, most of the time.'

'That tells me nothing.'

'No—and maybe it's less than fair. If it hadn't been for
Jean, you wouldn't still be walking the world.'

'She was good to me. I can't see what she had to gain from
it.'

'Just say she was good. It's a word some people still use.'

'But I don't see where she fits in,' Anne said.

'It was her job to clear off with you, make sure you were
delivered back whole. To look after you until Edwin paid up.'

'But something went wrong with the job?'

'I've told you: your father didn't want you back.'

'So why will he want me back now?'

'Publicity. His image. I'll admit it depends on how we play
it—on how *you* play it. We might have to write up your
memoirs for the press: to persuade him to offer us more than
they do.'

'When did you first meet my mother?'

'When we were both on the loose. She was on the run, on
her uppers, one last gutter-stone removed from being on the
game. A chance came up—and we both took it. I was on my
uppers, too—*and* on the game. I gave Jean her chance.'

'Was Len the father of your baby?'

'What baby?'

'You were Stella Davidge, weren't you? Of Northwood
Hills? Your father was an assessor of fire insurance. You were
sixteen when—'

'I don't know what you're on about.'

But Anne knew she had scored. Angela went out slamming
the door.

★

When you are reading *Who's Who*, you have to remember that men write their own entries. That is the key to interpreting them.

Edwin Booth was born in 1916, a war baby: but he did not seem to want his public to know anything of his parentage. Nor about his education, which he summed up as *continuing*. There was something bleak, too, about the notes on his marriages.

1) 1953, Diane, *née* Keightley, d.1959.

2) 1959 Alison Sarah, *née* Reyckaerts.

No reference to a daughter of the first marriage, presumably no issue of the second. Most of the entry was a catalogue of his works: author of four million words—to date. *Puppets at Noon* (1935) was the first, probably undergraduate glitter. But if he had been to university, why not name it? *Four Marys*, (1956). The major works often had biblical or near-biblical titles, starting with the big one, 1953, *Son of Nimshi*, which had brought him his first substantial shekels. Then came one a year for a few years, including his *Little Wars* trilogy: *Up River*, *Up Country* and *Sheba's Consul*. This was said to take the lid off a scabrous colonial slice. Booth dissected pop history, and history was sex: epochs had been fashioned by unfinished orgasms and stultified erections. Prime ministers and pro-consuls lived lives of driving sexuality that perhaps owed something to Booth's own masturbatory daydreams. *Translated into fourteen languages—seven major films—*

He was a prig, too: *Recreation: writing. Clubs: none.*

Kenworthy had tried to read a Booth novel, a purported lid-lifter about the General Strike, showing that the real defeat of the Unions had taken place in sundry beds—the proletariat banned from their own by hungry wives, TUC functionaries falling to seducers put up by cabinet and press. Booth's books were not so much to a formula as to a rhythm. Every five pages the veins of a man's face were laid bare: every four a penis rose, a vulva hung heavy, nipples crept.

Kenworthy turned to Basset's form-sheet. He had been

born in 1937, had been to prison twice: for six months in 1962 for a post-office hold-up in County Durham, and then again for a year in 1966 for uncomplicated burglary. He must have got away with a good deal of undetected activity, which argued that he was pretty efficient.

So how had he set about tracking Jean Cossey? How had he followed her to Broadstairs? The trouble with the Criminal Record Office was that it did not help with crimes a man got away with. That was where Kenworthy's department was going to come in: provided they had fed in the right trigger-factors.

Why had Basset not traced Jean to London when she moved down from Lancashire? What new green light had prompted her to move—since Basset was still at large? Why had it been Anne's wedding that had set off the last act? And why had they had to get Jean Cossey out of the way?

And what was the point of asking any question that did not lead them within the next few hours to Anne Lawson?

The key in the door again. Anne was afraid that Basset might come up alone. But it was Angela again, smiling with brazen insincerity and carrying a drinks tray.

'There's gin, Scotch, Martini.'

'I'm quite sure I'm not supposed to—'

'Have it your own way. How's that side of you, by the way?'

It would not be true to say that she was better: she did not know whether she was better or not. What she did know was that she had gone for some hours without the worst of her symptoms. Angela beat about no bushes.

'So. You've got on to something big. You know I used to be Stella Davidge. She was a girl who had committed no crimes—except against the statute book of Northwood Hills.'

'It struck me when I read about you,' Anne said. 'You'd more than a fair share of rotten luck.'

'Your luck is what you make of it.'

'Perhaps.'

'But this intrigues me, Anne. How would you like it if eighteen forgotten years of your life suddenly came back and clobbered you?'

'Isn't that roughly what's happening to me too?'

'If you like. But nobody's got the sort of file on you that evidently exists about me.'

'I'll trade you—I'll trade you any information you like for what you can tell me about Jean Cossey.'

Angela looked at her with that conviction of superior, hard-case worldliness that had characterized their first meeting in Jean Cossey's flat.

'And who's to guarantee that either of us is telling the truth?'

'That's a chance we've both got to take, isn't it? After all, we each know *something*—and the other doesn't know what.'

'All right. I'll tell you. Jean and I met when we were about as far down in London as you can get—and still stay alive. When you hit that low, there are a few places left that you can still go to, a few rounds you can still make. Sally Army. *Some* soup-kitchens: but you have to stay out of the claws of the do-gooders. And you keep seeing the same people's faces all over the place: railway refreshment rooms—till they move you on. It stands to sense, the dirtier you begin to look, the less chance you have. But some kind sod will always leave a bit of pie-crust on a plate, half a dozen cold chips.'

Outside, a high-perched bird was issuing his last territorial challenge of the day.

'Jean was slick at grabbing from tables that hadn't been cleared. She was different from me—more practical—in some ways, not in others. I wasn't keen on saddling myself with her at first. Even when we were slithering about on the crappiest of bottoms, she couldn't think higher than still wanting to be a groupie. She lived and slept for pop music. I kept promising myself I'd cut loose from her. But my God, she was quick at nicking morsels of food! And she was good with the kid—*my* kid—don't forget I was still lumbered.'

'What happened to him?'

'Her. She had to go when I teamed up with Len. And I'd no sense of loss by that time, I can tell you. It was Jean who felt that pinch. She'd been seeing more of the kid than I had.'

'But you'd stuck out so fiercely against having her adopted.'

'There are two ways of learning sense, and one of them's harder than the other. Besides, it all depended on who was trying to do the insisting. Jean was besotted with the child. She got besotted over all kinds of things. I was living in a grotty bed-sit in Notting Hill—and it's a wonder I got that. But nothing's impossible down-town—if you can find a way of paying for it. I managed to make a few quid in the only way that was open to me—but even for that, you have to have what amounts to a union card. I had to keep off the regulars' beats, and there were some uncompromising types watching the corners where it was all happening.'

A certain amusement had come into her eyes.

'My God, was I green! I had to learn things that I'd never dreamed of. Like doing all you can to make a man shed his load before he gets at you. It saves wear and tear.'

Her momentary wish was to disgust Anne, and Anne was determined not to be disgusted. It was the first time she had come up one to one against someone who had actually lived the life. She looked as neutral as she could.

'Shaking you, am I? It shook Jean. Once she tried to sermonize me out of it. But when she'd finished saying what she had to say, I quietly passed her her babysitting whack. And I've got to say she was a brick. Anyone would have thought the kid was hers. People *did* think the kid was hers. Sometimes I didn't see the pair of them for a week at a time. That was after Len came into the picture. I'd had to face up to the fact that I needed my own strong man, or my own corner. But Len said the kid had to go—and Jean cried her idiotic eyes out.'

'You mean, you had her officially adopted?'

'Official adoption's not easy. People ask questions. I left that side of things to Len. He knew people who could cut corners. Of course, it was given out to be Jean's kid.'

'But that must have meant papers, surely?'

'I don't know quite what they did about that—but papers were no problem. Len knew where to go. And he had to get on with it: he was putting the big job together at this time. It needed a lot of thinking out. Things were at what they call a sensitive stage. For one thing, I had to be got on the inside: nursemaid. That was where a spot of Northwood Hills double-talk didn't come amiss. More papers, references this time. And answers to them, when they were taken up. But Len had friends who could manage that. And things took on a different colour, when Edwin Booth set eyes on me. Mind you, there still had to be a bit of play-acting to get me past Diane. God, what a time it was when I moved in up Father Thames: having to keep my end up with Edwin and Len both. It was a good job I'd had a few weeks training. And Jean was waiting on the outside, to do the minding while Edwin was raking up the ransom. But you, damn you, were the one who nearly blew it. There was nothing you liked so much as to swing on a swing. Then you had to go and slip off the seat in mid-air. You came down on a snag, gashed yourself under a shoulder-blade. I wasn't looking—Diane nearly gave me the push over it. And that's the scar Len was trying to photograph—only there isn't enough of it. We shall have to think up something better than that. Edwin Booth's going to ask you some smart questions. Now it's your turn. What do you know about me?'

'There's a file on you.'

'Obviously. And how come you've seen it?'

'That's my job—updating old records.'

'And how come you were working on this one? What's so

special about my file that it's had to be dug out?'

'They've been looking up children who went missing at the same time as I was kidnapped.'

'Who's *they*? Who's doing the looking?'

'Mainly a man called Kenworthy.'

'I dare say Len will have heard of him. What line is he taking?'

'How should I know? I'm a junior clerk.'

'No kidding? A principal in the action? This Kenworthy character has turned your insides out, hasn't he? Don't try to be clever. OK. So the Stella Davidge file has come up. So how many others have? So why should Stella Davidge stick in your mind? That's what I'm asking.'

'I don't know. Maybe something caught Kenworthy's eye. He's a man who doesn't tell you what's really on his mind. He simply had me in to see what I could remember.'

'And how much did you tell him?'

'How much could I tell him? How much could I remember? Those trees in front of this house. All the rest is blank.'

'It had better not stay blank much longer. You've got to remember a lot of things when you talk to your father.'

'The only thing that's come back is a blue-bird swinging from the ceiling.'

'Yes. You never did care for that bird. I used to threaten you with it. But we've got to have you doing better than a bird.'

CHAPTER 18

Swannee Foster was one of the acknowledged aristocrats. It was generally understood that he would need to do something uncharacteristically lax before he'd have to surrender to his bail for it.

Like Lionel Friedman, Swannee had done one spell inside. The establishment is notorious for coming down heavily on those who counterfeit its national bank's promises to pay. That had been just before the war. Eighteen months later, Swannee was released to do some creative work for MI14, that sub-compartment of Military Intelligence which concerns itself with supporting escapes from prisoner-of-war compounds. Suitably guided and grubstaked, Swannee became adept at producing *Wehrmacht* passes, travel warrants on German trains, *Besatzung* chits authorizing circulation after curfew, and labour permits for foreign workers within Hitler's fortress.

Even in his ultimate civilian freedom, Foster had occasionally been called in to produce misleading printed papers. When an undercover trio from the Sweeney had had to be shoe-horned into labouring jobs on construction sites, it had been Swannee who had provided their stamped-up insurance cards. The Yard could have got them direct from the DHSS, but Swannee's deliveries were quicker, his questions were fewer—and there was decidedly less likelihood of leakage.

The order did not exist in writing to leave Swannee alone—but Swannee was left alone. It was one of the uncharted traditions of the Yard. His sources of livelihood were not documented. And indeed, as the years passed, his infringements of the law became fewer as they became more lucrative—except, perhaps, for the odd personal favour.

Like most of the upper few, Swannee was conscious of the blue nuances in his bloodstream that distinguished him from those who might have liked to pass themselves off as his peers. It offended Swannee when some claimant to his class of nobility failed to live up to his feudal obligations. Swannee had a comprehensive knowledge of the heraldry and alliances of the lesser breeds—and a supreme contempt for all of them. There were some offences for which he had undisguised scorn. Time had proved him not beyond dropping scalding hints when he felt that someone had earned a spell in Coventry.

Dialogues with Swannee were apt to be cryptic and elliptical. Kenworthy went to see him at his home in Royal Berkshire: the sort of establishment that looked from the road like an exclusive stud. And, in fact, he did keep a trainer and a small string, though he had never made turf history. It would, indeed, have embarrassed Swannee to have received any kind of public acclaim. Swannee was not a horsey man, and his life had none of the complications of a horsey man's. But his stabling and paddocks gave him a *raison d'être*. They also gave him buildings that could house other things besides horses, as well as space and an envelope.

He received Kenworthy in his library. He spent a good deal of his time reading—mostly very specialized matter. Swannee did not care to think that any man knew more than he did about some of the finer aspects of printing He greeted Kenworthy cordially.

'I've been expecting you, Chief Superintendent.'

'Yes. I hope you were not too hard on Lionel. I did lean on him rather heavily.'

'You did him a good turn. That son of his was making a mistake. He's pulled out of the video trade, Lionel promised me. He ought to have known better.'

'I'll not waltz about the point, Swannee. I'm going back some years, and I need to know how Jean Cossey got hold of birth certificates. You'll know all about Jean Cossey. She's been in the news. I'm not quite sure what name she used when she came to see you.'

. Swannee did not try to dissimulate.

'The goodness of my heart,' he said. 'I should have listened to my old mother. Time and again she told me never to do favours. The only trouble I've ever been in my life was through trying to be a boy scout.'

Kenworthy waited, glancing up at Swannee's shelves. There were in-folio editions here such as university libraries receive from royal bequests.

'Some chit of a girl messes up her life. She needs a bit of paper to square things up for her. It filled an interesting hour for me. So has society really suffered over that?'

Swannee knew that his standing was good with higher ranks than Kenworthy's. No one was going to pull him in for Jean Cossey's certificates.

'You should have forged the blanks as well as the calligraphy.' Kenworthy said. 'And why the hell didn't you make them certified copies? Why do it the hard way, with fake originals?'

'Don't know. Made the job more interesting, I suppose. More of a challenge.'

'And now Jean Cossey's dead. What can you tell me about that?'

Swannee gave it some thought. He was a little man, who kept his white hair close-cropped. He gave the impression of a weathered life, though except for an occasional horsey-looking walk across the downs, he spent most of his hours indoors, peering closely at detail.

'Somebody's building up to something,' he said at last.

'Such as selling the girl back to her father?'

'It could be that.'

'What I don't understand,' Kenworthy said, 'is how they think they can get away with that, when it was they who took her in the first place.'

'*They?*'

'Don't try to outsmart me, Swannee. You know very well you once tried to get Sid Heather to put it down to Len Basset.'

'Did I? I don't remember. It doesn't sound very likely to me. Maybe Sid got hold of the wrong end of the stick.'

As an argument, he did not intend that this should be taken seriously. But there was something of an edge of scalpel steel in Foster's tone, indicating that he had said all he was going to say. It was an unindexed ingredient of the Swannee

legend that the pull he could exercise in high places could
start an avalanche. He had helped in his time in other ways,
besides national insurance cards.

'Things have changed, Mr Kenworthy.'

'Nothing's changed, Swannee.'

'No, well—there are two ways of looking at most things.
I'll ask a few questions up and down, I promise you that. And
I'll find some way of getting in touch. I don't want you
coming here again, Mr Kenworthy.'

He spoke in the tone of a man accustomed always to make
his own terms.

Detective-Sergeant Lawson lingered at the end of a briefing
session waiting for a word with Wright.

'Is anything happening at all, sir?'

Wright looked at him with eyes that were beginning to
show signs of too many hurried snacks, too little exercise, not
enough sleep.

'You know as much as I do, Howard.'

The car which had picked up the invalid chair at Shortlands Station had been properly booked in at the BR car
park: its driver must have wanted to avoid any scrapes with
even minor officials. The top ranks seemed to think it
impossible that that car should have been driven out of Kent.
Wright's squad was dealing in depth with a very narrow
sector.

'I've every right to be put where the action is,' Lawson
said.

'Be your age, Howard. You know damned well no such
right exists. And when it comes to personal involvement,
there's only one attitude that prevails at the summit. And I
agree with that attitude. You know that too.'

'Yes, sir, but—'

'Well, tell me, then—what line ought we to be following?'

What could Howard say? That he had a gut feeling? That
the answer might lie somewhere among the airy notions that

Anne had in her head? In dreams, and wisps of memory?

'I know it's difficult, sir.'

But Wright seemed loath to let it go at that.

'Howard—suppose I said, "Right—free-lance. Go where you want, and follow up anything your nose runs into." Which way would you head?'

'I don't know.'

'How much leave have you owing to you?'

'None. Spain took up every half-day I had in credit.'

'I suppose you could go sick: *depression*.'

'Don't want that on my record.'

'Nor would I. So concentrate on what you're doing. Your job is to keep a guiding eye on a dozen DC's and aides with their questionnaires.'

Commander Cawthorne had turned his conference room into an operations centre that looked as if he were all set to repel airborne invasion. A map of the kingdom had been pinned across accumulated tables. Counters representing provincial help could be thrust up and down with implements that looked uncommonly like billiard-rests borrowed from *Recreation*. The last sighting of Anne Lawson was still shown as a railway station between Bromley and Beckenham.

Kenworthy went through the proper channels and asked to see Cawthorne.

The evening was fading. After a three-hour session, Angela had gone downstairs—turning the key behind her, though nothing could have been friendlier between them. There were, in fact, at least three Angelas. There was the woman who had lived her own life, had learned all the lessons there were to be learned—and who treated Anne as she had treated her in Jean Cossey's flat: with a smug and lofty cynicism. There was the woman who reminisced racily about her transition from Stella Davidge to Basset's right-hand woman. And there was a third creature, God knows how false, who nevertheless appeared to be Anne's friend.

Angela had brought her magazines: next month's *Homes and Gardens* and a miscellany of paperbacks ranging from Penguin Crime to a Deep South saga that Edwin Booth would not have disowned.

Outside, the trees were being drained of colour in what seemed an abnormally still twilight. Angela had said that she would be back with something for bedtime. From the lower regions of the house came the rise and fall of indistinguishable voices: a radio or TV play. Something had moved through the vegetation in the orchard under the window: some nocturnal hunter coming to life, perhaps a cat reverting to nature.

Now Anne had a new dilemma. The way things had gone, she had drifted into a mindless co-operation with Angela. Did any alternative exist? Did this ludicrous situation itself exist?

Could Edwin Booth possibly have been her father? Everything she had gleaned about the Booths suggested that she would find them totally unsympathetic. But then Angela—whose role in the whole business had been nothing better than shamelessly criminal—could hardly be looked on as an unprejudiced reporter.

Angela confidently expected that Anne would be meeting her father within the next forty-eight hours. That was not something to which Anne could give proper credence. Trying to recharge Anne's memory, Angela had talked a lot about the old days in the Thames Valley, about walks in the water-meadows, about how Anne, even at the age of two and a half, had insisted to the point of superstition on always following exactly the same sequence of footpaths. Every afternoon had had to follow a ritually undeviating pattern—talking through gaps in the hedge to the same cattle, patrolling the perimeter of the grounds in the same order, throwing crusts to the ducks, all of which she knew by name, knowing precisely which shallows under the bank minnow fry were to be seen. Angela came out of it, even at this range of time, as a bored companion—bored to dementia by the child, jealous of the child's quality of life, doing no more than keep up the minimal appearance needed to hang on to her job. How infatuated had Edwin Booth been with her—or did it even amount to an infatuation? The way Angela talked about it, it seemed more like a series of acts of sexual evacuation. And what picture emerged of Anne's mother? She came out of Angela's talk as no more than a spoiled sex-kitten of whom her husband had grown tired, bored by the facility with which she had always been given everything she had ever asked for.

'Look, Angela,' Anne said. 'This is all very well. You know it's driving me to distraction not remembering a thing. But all you're telling me is the things I did when you were supposed to be looking after me. What about relations between me and my parents?'

She was beginning to suspect that this was something that Angela would not know much about.

'As far as I could see, that didn't amount to much,' Angela said. 'Your father was working and must not be disturbed. Your mother had friends in, or was out visiting—Marlborough, Oxford, the West End. Or resting and not to be bothered.'

'That's not going to help me to impress Edwin Booth, is it? There's barely a word I can say that will persuade him I'm who you say I am. Didn't anything *real* ever happen? Didn't I sometimes have to be punished for misbehaving at table? Or wasn't I even allowed to eat with them?'

'As a rule I gave you your meals in the nursery. And of course there'd been a Nanny before me. You were usually expected to go round the grown-ups and say good night.'

'Great! Didn't I even get a bedtime story?'

'Usually from me.'

'They must have been beauties. Did you start giving me my first lessons in contraception?'

'There's no need to be like that.' Angela said. 'Now I come to think about it, bedtime stories are something that might be worth pursuing. I remember major rows about your bedtime stories. You always preferred your father,'s, but he worked to a rigid routine, and your bedtime always came just as he was settling down to do his day's revision. Whatever you think about his books, he worked like a steam-hammer at them.'

'That's obvious from his output.'

'But if he was in the right mood—which wasn't often—he would tell you a story, made-up on the spur of the moment, and running on like a serial. And you were a demanding little thing. Let him forget a detail from yesterday, let him forget somebody's name, and you came down on him like a ton of bricks. But as I say, this didn't happen often. He was more likely to send you off to your mother for a story. And she'd maybe send you back to him. "You can write books for the pulp-mills," she'd say. "Can't you find five minutes for your own flesh and blood?"'

'But can't you fill me in some detail? What sort of stories did he tell me? What were they *about*?'

'How the hell should I know what they were about? Your mother read you stories out of books, if you were lucky. *Goldilocks*, *The Wizard of Oz*. But you could see her yawning. She'd miss bits out to get the thing over more quickly, and you used to get uptight about that. Sometimes she'd fling the book across the room before she got to the end of it.'

'Had I any toys?'

'*Any* toys? We could have opened a shop.'

'The only toys I can remember are the ones Jean Cossey bought me.'

'You had an old doll's house, a priceless period piece. I once played with it for an hour myself—only you kept getting in my way.'

'Which toys were my favourites?'

'Oh, the usual thing—the rag, tag and bobtail. You had a stuffed animal of some sort or other. You'd chewed the dye out of its ears when you were in the teething stage, and it was taken off you because it was unhygienic. You created and wouldn't go to bed without it.'

'What did I call it?'

'You expect me to know that? And that's pointless, anyway—because Edwin Booth wouldn't know its name. I doubt if he knew it existed. Now if you could remember some of the things you heard said when he and Diane were having rows—that might convince him.'

'It's hopeless,' Anne said. 'I can't even remember *them*, let alone the things they said.'

'No—but I might be able to remember for you. I promise you—I'll be working on it.'

Anne had no patience for any more of this. They did not persevere after that. Angela went downstairs and said she would be back later. After she had gone, Anne thought of another possible line of approach: her friends. She must have been friends with other children. Surely she'd sometimes been invited to parties. She must have had other kids in to play in that garden.

She went and drew her curtains. Outside, it looked like an invigorating spring night. It was a shame to shut it out, a pity to be indoors. It did not seem to her that she would ever be free again.

She heard the creak of a landing floorboard, and someone was having trouble with a key in her door. It did not strike her at first that it would be anyone but Angela, paying her last visit of the day. But it was Basset who came in, wearing a sheeny and flamboyant dressing-gown that might have been designed for the wartime Churchill. His hair was damp-plastered down as after a shower, and he had clearly been drinking. His speech was thick and he was having to think about his words. As he turned to lock the door behind himself, he swayed for a moment almost off-balance.

'So—Angie tells me that your homework is not up to much.'

'My homework?'

'You've not been remembering like a little girl should.'

'If I can't remember, I just can't. It's no use flogging the horse any harder.'

He came close to where she was standing.

'I suppose we shall hear next that you don't even remember me. I was around from time to time. Have you forgotten how we used to like each other, oh so long ago?'

There was something treacly in his tone that sickened rather than frightened her. He was a man who did not believe that the woman lived who would not find him irresistible.

'You had a roving eye for passing males when you were two,' he said. 'You had a way of smiling at men that showed you had a future.'

He seized her wrists and pulled her towards him. When she tried to draw away, he tightened his grip so that it hurt.

'You know—you've developed.'

'Let me go.'

'And you had to go and throw yourself away on a London copper.'

'I shall scream for Angela.'

He laughed. 'You think she cares?'

He let go of her left hand, but only to crook his arm round her waist and pull her tight to him. She kicked his shins, and that seemed to make no impression on him. He was a powerful man, and her struggling only had her worse immobilized.

'Go on, then—scream for Angela. She'll laugh her head off.'

She did scream, and her mouth, wide open, was close to his ear. He let go of her wrist to clap his hand crudely over her lips.

Angela must still be in the house. She would surely not stand for this.

'Now listen—'

With her free hand she flew at his face, furrowing deep downward scratches. But it did her no good. He got her wrists together and gripped them agonizingly.

'Calm down, lady.'

CHAPTER 19

Kenworthy had to wait to see Cawthorne. He had to wait first for an answer to his request for an appointment, and when that message eventually tracked down from the secretary, the interview was put off until late in the day. And when Kenworthy went up, he was kept hanging about in an ante-room.

The hostility between Kenworthy and Cawthorne went a long way back in time. It was true that there were faults on both sides, but they were not evenly balanced between the sides. It was a relationship that brought out the least useful features of both men. And on the infrequent occasions on which they had to collaborate, they always both became less than fully effective. Today, Cawthorne was playing the game of being joyful to see a subordinate. It was a meaningless act.

'I know I was warned,' Kenworthy opened. 'I know I've been trespassing—'

'In the heat of the moment, Simon, we sometimes say things that we don't really mean. Anyone who comes up here to shed a little light on this matter is well met.'

Kenworthy let this bland hypocrisy pass by on his blind side. Cawthorne was obviously disposed to a spell of brain-picking.

'Take this, for example. I can't think why your bosom friend Wright hasn't moved heaven and earth to find this woman.'

He passed Kenworthy a typescript report, headed

HALLAM, Angela. It emanated from the uniform branch of the Lewisham division.

'Before you read it, you might as well know, Simon, that I've pushed this inquiry down to station level of every force in the country. Angela Hallam—where is she? And more to the point: where was she while the Cossey woman was being electrocuted? Well—we know the answer to the second question now. She was in the company of our Lewisham friends.'

Angela Hallam had driven her Triumph Toledo out of a side-road into the near-side headlamp of a van that she claimed not to have seen. Therefore she was told that she would be reported for a potential without-due-care-and-attention charge. The taking of statements was done in leisurely fashion, and provided her alibi, well away from Jean Cossey's bathroom. The critical time was very adequately accounted for.

'In fact,' Kenworthy said, 'this establishes her as the murderer.'

'Does it now?'

'Yes. If you can put your hands on who it was that stood in for her in Lewisham—complete with her driving licence, certificates of insurance and MoT test. She will, of course, answer the summons herself.'

'They've been to the address in Putney that the woman gave. There was no one about, milk and papers cancelled, no local knowledge of her whereabouts. But it was undoubtedly Angela Hallam's flat: all sorts of telling evidence about that.'

'This will be the second time that this bunch have used law and order as their main cover.'

'What do you know, Simon?'

'That a man called Basset could not have kidnapped a child by the Upper Thames because he was doing a post-office in County Durham at the time. At least, the evidence said that Basset did the post-office; and he quite happily did bird for it.'

'*Modus operandi*. It's the opposite of clever to repeat a pattern, just because it worked once.'

'It's clever enough, if you can make it work twice.'

'This is going to be difficult,' Cawthorne said.

'So I suggest you don't waste time trying to break these alibis. That's not where you'll nail them.'

But at this point Cawthorne was called into his campaign HQ. Kenworthy followed him in as if he had been invited. Someone had moved a red counter to a new location in southern England: the latest report had come in about the movements of Edwin Booth, novelist.

You had to give Cawthorne his due for thoroughness. The moment Booth had made his first move from Jersey, officers of the island force were on the move too. As Booth's Cessna homed in on the Lizard, air-controllers' plottings were being translated into visual symbols on Cawthorne's operational table.

The plane landed on a club strip on the outskirts of Falmouth, having been delayed for the spell of a stacking circuit while an ace couple from the Cornwall CID reported themselves in position. Booth, an unmistakable bear-like man, drove a hired Sierra eastwards while his pilot made his way to an inn. After the Tamar bridge a couple of unobtrusive Devonians took over, and on the Exeter by-pass were replaced by a squad under Cawthorne's direct jurisdiction. They worked in staggered pairs, in radio contact with each other and their base, so that Booth did not urinate in a lay-by without a report going to Cawthorne.

The bear-like man overnighted in The Rose and Crown at Salisbury, and the register was duly signed *Booth*. A new leap-frogging team had him in sight the next morning through Andover and Basingstoke, where he took the A339 south. He stopped for lunch at The Angel at Midhurst, then afterwards drove in leisurely fashion across Sussex, finishing his day in Lewes, where he registered under the new name of Rawdon. Here he craftily managed to get into conversation with two of his shadows, who were forthwith replaced by strangers: Cawthorne's mobile cadre was geared for flexible action.

The next morning, the man giving himself out to be Rawdon was on his way to Newhaven to catch the Dieppe boat. He had told the two men in the bar that he had a thing about flying. And since they must at all costs conceal their knowledge of how he had arrived at Falmouth, this did not lead to a conversational trap. Rawdon did take the Dieppe boat, and Interpol was activated.

The cost in time and manpower was lavish. The message that had just reached the report centre as Kenworthy followed Cawthorne in was that another bear-like man, this time carrying a British passport in the name of Booth, had arrived in Southampton on the Sea-Link ferry. Cawthorne's machine had made ample allowances for shunts and loop-ways.

'So Booth wants to play it his own way,' Cawthorne said.

'As he did once before.'

'And he's recruited skilled help.'

'Seems so.'

Cawthorne looked at Kenworthy keenly.

'Simon, far be it from me to want to seem churlish. You have been very helpful. But there is something that has to be said.'

They were in the deciding round at last. Kenworthy knew that he was on the carpet. The interesting thing was the form that the carpeting was taking. Cawthorne was being too nice about it—wrapping things up, keeping Kenworthy sweet. So all that mattered was the message of the moment. The current state of play between two old enemies was of lesser importance.

'Simon, I know you want in on this. I see no real difficulty in letting you in. No problem. I want this thing knotted and sealed.'

'I can see only one way in,' Kenworthy started to say.

'There's one thing I must ask you.'

'What's that?'

Kenworthy snapped it out. Here came the crux of the matter, and he knew in advance that it was a crux that he would be unwilling to accept. Cawthorne's entire demeanour was leading up to the unacceptable.

'Leave Swannee Foster to somebody else. Don't go visiting the downs again.'

'It makes me sick,' Kenworthy said—and it did. So Foster had put in a complaint—and it had been listened to.

'It makes me wonder what hold Swannee's got over us.'

'Over *me*, do you mean?'

The Commander looked as if he were about to protest too much. Kenworthy knew Cawthorne well. He believed he could see through every shade and phase of his bluff and his play-acting, of his sales-talk and his deals from under the pack. But Cawthorne at this moment was trying to do something unusual. He was trying to convince Kenworthy of a truthful fact.

'Simon—it's no secret that I've used methods in my time that you wouldn't. I've cut corners in ways that I wouldn't care to have publicized. But I've never connived at injustice. Not once in my career. The opposite. If I had not taken the course of action that I've chosen once or twice, there are odd bits of justice that never would have got done. You know what I'm talking about.'

Kenworthy did. He knew that if certain facts ever came to light about planting evidence—against men of known but unprovable guilt—Cawthorne would have gone the way taken by a number of senior officers in recent times. The question that mattered to Kenworthy was not whether justice had been done—it was not even whether Cawthorne would have got his promotions otherwise. It was that Cawthorne never questioned his own judgement of what was just and what was unjust. In fact Cawthorne had never cared. All that he had ever lived for was showing results: not *getting* them—*showing* them.

'Never in my career have I owed anything to Swannee Foster. Others may have.'

It was a landmark in the wars between Kenworthy and Cawthorne. Cawthorne was speaking the truth—and Kenworthy was believing him.

'Who?'

'Don't ask.'

'I bloody well hate this. I've hated the Yard since—'

'Bide your time, Simon. That's what I'm doing. Make the most of the passing moment. It *is* passing.'

'One visit from me, and he's begging for protection. And getting it. What's he scared of?'

But Cawthorne moved pointedly to a new subject.

'Foster apart, who else would you like to talk to?'

Kenworthy thought for a few seconds.

'I'd like to go up to Lancashire.'

'Lancashire?'

'There's a girl called Gwen Beecham. If you could get me clearance—'

'Act as if you've already got it.'

'That'll make a change—doing something according to the book.'

Howard Lawson saw his DCs and aides off on their designated routes. He also picked out the senior detective-constable and told the others that if they lighted on anything and he did not happen to be around, this man would do the necessary liaison with Shiner. He made it sound as if this were a perfectly normal way of conducting a detective-sergeant's business.

Lawson knew in theory that love between a man and a woman was not static. What he had not expected was that his feelings for Anne should have altered so much in the short time since they had flown from Gatwick to Faro: though the interval was not to be considered normal by anyone's standards.

Now he was cut off from her, hopelessly cut off. There was one lethal fact to be faced: one tiny mistake by those who were supposed to know what they were doing, and Anne was likely to lose her life. He could not hang about, not doing anything about it himself.

This was the sort of bedrock thought that changed a man's attitudes—and that did not just mean being sorry about a lunch-time scene in her office. He thought again about the whimsical things that she was always saying. His attitude and Anne's were different. When he had first met her, while they had been engaged, he had enjoyed her fantasies as one might enjoy a light book at the end of a tiring day. He had never doubted her sincerity—but many of her ideas were simply fanciful. Now a cold grip of certainty had hold of him. All the odd things that she said had a beginning somewhere—a logical beginning, a reality. And the men at the bottom of this reality would be willing to kill to achieve their ends.

Take this Hobbema picture. Lawson had never seen a reproduction of it—not to know that that was what he was looking at. He knew it only from Anne's description, and had put the ingredients together in a different pattern from hers, producing a different picture.

Now he went to the National Gallery to look at the original.

He stood and looked at the *Avenue in Middleharnis*. Until he lost consciousness of the shuttle of shufflers, around, behind and in front of him. Anne had never been to Middleharnis: she had always stressed the difference between the dream and the painting itself. She had been somewhere like Middleharnis.

If only the sort of magic that Anne believed in were true, it ought to be possible to gaze at that painting and answer the question *Where?*—by taking thought, as Anne herself had once said in a different context.

And now Howard knew—without the need for magic. It was the Fens—Cambridgeshire, Lincolnshire. There had been an address in Lincolnshire, early in the log.

Waterman's Cottage, Spurlsby Drove, Lincs. That had been the address from which Jean Cossey had first written to the estate agent in Broadstairs.

Howard looked at the time. It was going to be a testing drive. He would be in dereliction of duty. He could not expect any support from Shiner if he came unstuck.

CHAPTER 20

Kenworthy and Bartram called on Gwen Beecham together. She lived in a nineteen-fiftyish close on the unfinished spec-built estate on the outskirts of Slodden-le-Woods.

There were two children. Gwen had had them somewhat later in her child-bearing life than some of her contemporaries had had theirs. Her fourteen-year-old boy had retreated upstairs to equal rations of homework and hard rock. Her eight-year-old was about the living-room and the floor was scattered with enough *Lego* to model Manhattan. Gwen Beecham must in her time have been an attractive young woman—perhaps more especially in the eyes of the unsophisticated. But she was no longer putting much effort into her appearance. Her hair was too long to keep itself tidy, her jeans were as she discarded them at night and picked them up in the morning. She had squirmed into her off-white sweater as it had come to hand. Her house was not badly kept, and she was not without possessions: a signed print or two, two shelves of Literary Guild, commonplace travel trophies from France, Denmark and the Algarve.

It was possible to judge that life had treated Gwen Beecham undeservedly badly. Of the three girls who had known each other in Stella Davidge's London, she was the one who had lived and gone on living in the YWCA, who had not had to dodge the claws of the do-gooders, who had not eaten discarded pie-crusts from other people's plates—who had not even liked talking of women being on the game. Then after more than fifteen years of conventionally faultless married life, her husband had left her, for no other reason, it seemed, than for a change of sexual partner. In the course of the usual machinery, she could expect to get such compensation as was considered her entitlement. It was not inconceivable that some fault of her own had contributed to the disaster. This was not Kenworthy's nor Bartram's business, and they steered round the dangers of going into it. But they were both experienced enough to know that the events of her life would influence her telling of events in other people's lives.

'So—what can you tell us about Jean Cossey? Well—you knew her as Jean other things—Pogson, for one.'

'Yes.'

Gwen Beecham leaned back her head, half closed her eyes and looked nostalgically remote. She became nostalgically remote several times during the course of the evening that Bartram and Kenworthy spent with her.

'She was a strange girl, very likable, though unmanageable at times. Of course, she should never have left home. She should never have fallen out with her parents. They should never have allowed themselves to fall out with her. She should have gone back to see them. She should have made things up with them. I kept telling her to. I don't know whether it was pride or shame or conscience that stopped her. I'm beginning to think nowadays that even conscience is an illusion.'

'How long had she been in London before you saw which way things were going with her?'

'She turned up without notice. It shattered me. I know I'd written her letters that had made her want to come. But then, you write people letters about the things that interest them, don't you? Pop groups, lead guitarists, road managers—that was all she had in her head. I mean, we all went through it to some extent, I suppose. But Jean didn't seem as if she was ever going to go on to anything else. There was even a time when she fancied herself as a singer.'

'But she did at least grow out of that?'

'She had an audition with some amateurs. I think it was Balham, or Tooting. When they played the recording back to her, it was enough to cure anyone.'

Gwen Beecham was out of the laughing habit. The smile that she mustered up was rudimentary and short-lived.

'Surely she'd heard a recording of her own voice before?'

'Not with backing.'

'And the life she was leading didn't appeal to you?'

'She couldn't find work. She spent a lot of time hanging about squalid dance-halls—getting there early, so that she could see the group set their gear up. It was worse than flirting—she was throwing herself at them. As far as they were concerned, she was just another—luckily for her, I always thought.'

'So she didn't actually take up with any of them?'

'She *said* she did. But I didn't believe half her stories. She knew what to say to upset me. And I let her know I wasn't interested in the sort of people she was trying to take up with. I thought I'd better make that clear early on. This was the time of the Rock 'n' Roll riots. Gangs of youths went to dances all ready—tooled-up, they called it, with flick knives, even choppers.'

'Had she any friend in particular that you objected to?'

'There was Angela. I told you about her the other day, Mr Bartram.'

'How and where did she meet her?' Kenworthy asked.

'I can't tell you. By then she wasn't spending much time in my company.'

'What did you object to in Angela?'

'What pop was to Jean, sex was to Angela. It was the time when adolescent girls were wearing golliwogs from marmalade jars to show that they were no longer virgins. Angela didn't just wear her golliwog—she made sure you didn't miss it.'

'Did Jean wear one?'

'Sometimes, I think, but she took it off to come into the hostel.'

'Did you know that Angela had already had a baby?'

'Not at first. And then I didn't believe it straight away. It came up in the conversation as if they thought I'd known all along.'

'So who was looking after the child when Jean and Angela were out together?'

'I've got a horrible feeling that some of the time nobody was. Only it upset Jean to think of her being neglected. And she started taking care of her herself. I tell you, Jean was a mixture.'

'You knew that at the time she was doing it? You hadn't completely broken off with her?'

'I tried not to lose touch altogether. I thought I'd be some sort of anchorage for her, even if we only saw each other for an hour now and then.'

'You must have been a very hopeful young person. You know what we're trying to get at, don't you, Gwen?'

'Not really.'

'I'm trying to pinpoint the day when those two girls' fortunes changed.'

'They went a long way down before that happened. They began to look dirty, smelled as if they'd given up taking baths. They told revolting stories of the things they were up to. I felt sure they were exaggerating, just to disgust me. Then things changed, as you say. And I can tell you exactly when it was. I'd taken things into my own hand, written to Jean's mother, persuaded her parents to come one weekend. It wasn't my business, but no one else was going to make it theirs. Of course, it was fatal. I wished I'd let well alone.'

'Instead of a reunion, a stand-up row?'

'In the hostel. I'm afraid Mr and Mrs Pogson didn't have much clue. I don't think they saw through to how bad things really were. I mean, they'd heard of this kind of nastiness, but I don't think in their heart of hearts they could believe that Jean was really mixed up in it. And they went on about things that didn't matter all that much—like not liking Jean's hairstyle. They insisted on treating her as if she were still a child. And whatever else she was, she'd put childhood behind her. I could see that they were reviving all the old bitterness, even before they'd started. And to make matters worse—'

From the room upstairs, the throbbing bass of her son's LP's was penetrating downwards. It made conversation difficult, but Gwen seemed unaware of it.

'What made matters worse was that I could see that Jean and Angela had something on between them that day. They had tidied themselves up no end. They were watching the clock. Later that afternoon, they were going somewhere. Jean asked me if I had a map, and all I had was an ancient school atlas, which wasn't much good. She couldn't find the place she was looking for. But I was watching every little move that might tell me anything, and I know it was near that town with the race-course: Newbury, is it? And I didn't—and don't—know a thing about racing. But I know they don't have meetings on Sundays.'

'Did you see either of them again after they'd kept this appointment?'

'Only once. And what a transformation! They must have spent a fortune in Carnaby Street.'

'You didn't pick up any more than that?'

'No. Previously they'd always been boastful in an indirect sort of way. Now I got the impression that they didn't trust me with what was going on. They stopped coming. They didn't need me to shock and impress any more. I guessed they'd moved into a new circle. That's all I can tell you. They drifted out of my life, and I can't say I wasn't relieved. Jean and I exchanged Christmas cards, perhaps wrote a line or two on them, but that's all I ever heard from her until I had that desperate phone call from her in Broadstairs.'

Bartram and Kenworthy rounded off their day over pints in a mouldy-smelling lounge bar in which they were the only customers.

'So you're a wiser man now, are you, Simon?'

'Considerably. I now know who scripted and produced the Edwina Booth kidnapping. I can guess whom he hired for the rough stuff on the ground. It was a man called Basset, who'd been poncing on a girl called Angela. And Jean Cossey was brought in as the baby-minder for Stage Two. But there are some questions I can't answer yet. I think I know whose idea it would have been to mount that County Durham job, and see that Basset got done for it. It was a fine alibi, with a double twist to it, because Basset had already been grassed to Sid Heather as kidnapper-in-chief. That was very clever of Swannee Foster. I've no doubt he felt sure that that let him out. Well, so it has—up to now. He's the key to all this, Swannee Foster. Where I'm still not on course is how an operator like Swannee got as far from his true trade as this. I've always admired Swannee—as a craftsman.'

CHAPTER 21

Directly he turned into Spurlsby Drove, Howard Lawson knew what Anne meant. He was a man entirely unendowed with any sense of the supernatural, of the uncanny. He did not claim to have a rational explanation for everything—but he believed that rational explanations could always be found. Yet he had a feeling, too strong to ignore, that he was now entering Anne's dream. There was nothing flesh-tingling about it. Trees, ruts, sandy soil, a largish house and a converted row of cottages: these things could not by themselves hurt a man. But he knew that there might be eyes behind the windows of one of those dwellings that might have no goodwill towards strangers. So he backed out of the entrance to Spurlsby Drove in the manner of a man who has mistakenly turned into a cul-de-sac, parked his car some way away in a gateway, well concealed by foliage from observation from the Drove. He kept his head down and worked out a reconnaissance that would bring him as near as he could get to the large house without showing himself.

At the end of an hour he returned to his car better informed on several counts. He knew, now, for example, that the large house was in the hands of someone who gardened with fervour—and with a talent for regimentation. Fences, shed doors and herbaceous borders were plumblined in inspection order, like a battalion drawn up in line. Creosoting was fresh and punctilious. Such machinery as could be seen—a petrol-driven tiller in a lean-to store—was as gleaming clean as if fresh bought. Apart from the two houses, there seemed to be no signs of human life within the confines of the landscape. But though he had seen no one, he knew it likely that he had been observed by this time. The smaller house, the converted cottages, was said to be occupied by a retired professor of political economy. What sort of man would a professor of political economy be? Either a crank, or someone who could comment reasonably on his fellow creatures. Howard changed his tactics, went under close cover to the entrance to the Drove, then proceeded in open view up to the cottage of the emeritus academic.

It was an architect's conversion that had not completely obliterated the memory of what had existed before: three agricultural labourers' cottages which in the nineteenth century had probably been no more than hovels, and that even with such modernization as the new century had brought would have remained poky, dark and damp. But now the picture windows, the removal of tight, narrow staircases and the throwing out of kitchen and bathroom annexes had completed the sell-out from the labouring to the leisured class. The woman who opened the door to Howard was in her advanced forties—a buxom figure who looked as if she might live life for the sake of the things she found to laugh at. He wondered if perhaps the professor had married one of his students. The professor himself, Walter Fynes-Pym, was working at a small portable typewriter in a book-stacked study of which the door was open; perhaps he was a man from whom work did not demand seclusion. He was bald and looked desiccated, a man past the mid-seventy mark. Fynes-Pym was not known to the non-specialist public—he had never dabbled in pop politics. Howard had done enough rapid checking to discover that he was regarded as an experts' expert, who would not, for example, be called on for comment by the TV trivializers—but who might behind the scenes be asked for his advice about the recruitment of a think-tank. Yet Howard was not to find him without the common touch, and a man constantly finding new ways of relieving the tedium of the emeritus life. Clearly he did not want to miss a visitor, and got up from his desk to come and meet Howard, even before being told who he was.

Howard had toyed with various cover stories, leaving the final choice until he saw what his reception might be. The first exchanges seemed so sympathetic that he told Fynes-Pym who he was—not only CID, but also Anne's husband.

'So what trail has been blazed to Spurlsby Drove?'

'I'd be undermining myself if I told you that. But I will: a recurring dream of my wife's.'

The professor chuckled as John Betjeman might at the sight of a Victorian parados in a lower middle-class terrace.

'So they're wrong when they say there's no romance left for the likes of us?'

'I'm afraid this affair is very far removed from the realm of romance.'

'I apologize. That was putting it badly. My mind's wandering. I'm looking at it from a purely selfish angle—the angle of a man who lives here.'

Howard got up from his chair, went to the window and looked at the house at the end of the Drove. He got a full view of it from this angle—its thatch, its mansard windows, and the windows of the lower rooms above the level of a regimentally barbered hedge. And yet by standing back no more than a foot or so, one could observe without letting oneself be seen.

'Who lives there?'

'A man and his wife, quiet types. They've been there since before we came here—name of Stableford. I think they must have bought the place in the immediate post-war years, probably got it in a dilapidated state for a price that seems laughable today. We don't see much of them. They're not exactly hermits—not rude if you speak to them—but they don't really care for company, and they let that quietly be seen. I have even wondered if company's something they're afraid of. I'd call them non-showy apostles of the good life. He grows, cures and smokes his own tobacco. He gave me a fill of it one day. I fought shy of telling him that I felt constrained to throw that pipe away afterwards.'

'Do they often go away from here?'

'Never for more than the long inside of a day. They couldn't. They have too much livestock of one kind or another: a goat, geese, Muscovy ducks, and a cob in their paddock. They drive to town in a trap for their weekly shopping.'

'Do they have many visitors?'

'Rarely—but some. It's the visitors that make us think that there might be something in the stories that the Agnews told us.'

He laughed drily but with some abandon. There was a certain excitement in him. It was not exactly puerile, but a sort of sophisticated childishness, a foil perhaps to unemployed mental brilliance.

'The Agnews—they were the people from whom you—'

'Took over this place. That's right. They had stood out stubbornly against being rehoused. We thought we'd never be able to close the deal. A crafty pair, I couldn't help thinking: hung on until they were finally resettled in a seaside bungalow. But you must not let me wander, Sergeant. You're here on much more serious business than the Agnews.'

'Have you seen any recent visitors at the house?'

'We have. And that's the point I've been working up to. Do you mind if I return to the Agnews for a moment? We met them when we first looked over the place, and again when we came informally with an architect friend. They were quite extraordinarily hospitable—and a couple who never stopped talking. They had been weaving legends about that house over there for years. Everything they saw happening there, they turned into some sort of sinister story. They watched everything, imagined that all the comings and goings were spy stories, drug traffic, a cache from the takings from large-scale burglaries. They even seemed to be able to pull the dates to fit in with the stories they'd got from the newspapers. If you mentioned a sensational crime they reckoned they could tie it up with something they'd seen over at that house. I don't know what reading matter they indulged in—there's a mobile library comes round every week or two—but they certainly had strong tastes for the lurid.'

'And since you've been here, sir—have you seen the same sort of thing going on?'

'Oh, we make a point of looking for it, Jane and I. We were so amused, you see, by the Agnews, that ever since we came here we've done our best to carry on the tradition. It's a sort of competition between the pair of us. We've seen anarchist couriers, scab labourers brought here by trades union thugs to be tortured, escaped convicts, political refugees, illegal immigrants—all in the imagination, of course. And all faithfully in the wake of the Agnews. You can have no idea, Sergeant, of how remote this place is—how much one is thrown back on one's mental resources. But I'm sorry—I'm wasting your time.'

'Far from it. I'd like to hear more of your stories—and especially of the Agnews'. I'd like to hear more about the real people who've put some of your fancies into your mind.'

'Oh dear, Sergeant what a pity! This is going to spoil our game, you know. Our whole joy has been in not taking life seriously. It will be unpalatable even to joke about these things from now on. Some of the Agnews' stories really were hilarious—only perhaps not quite as far-fetched as some that Jane and I have invented. And what a job it would be to sort out originating fact from subsequent fiction! Yet there were things that didn't seem quite normal: a man arriving on a bicycle in the middle of the night; an old felt hat, blown about the Drove by the wind, the morning after that visit. But if that place over there has been a safe house all these years—I suppose that's the term you use for it—then it could not have been more adroitly handled. I mean, there have been incidents, and I'll try to remember some for you. They have happened over the years. Sometimes there have been long intervals between them. Only last night, we thought we *might* have heard a woman scream.'

'Over there, in the house?'

'It seemed so. But you know how it is with something as evanescent as a single scream, heard behind closed doors, while you are watching the shoot-out of a classic western on the box.'

'What time was this?'

'Well—when does the shoot-out of a classic western generally take place? Giving time for the final credits, a very few minutes before the nine o'clock news.'

'So there are visitors at the house at the moment?'

'We have seen none. We *thought* we heard a car on the Drove at an ungodly hour the other morning, but neither of us got up to look—precisely because of the ungodliness of the hour. And a car would not necessarily be sinister. Despite his pony and trap, Stableford does run an old banger. And he does make an occasional marketing trip, usually dragging a trailer with crates of hens in it, greenstuff in season, that sort of thing.'

And it was at this stage that the professor's wife inserted herself into the conversation.

'You know, Walter, it's very wrong indeed to be playing fox and geese with the Sergeant like this. He is not here to listen to small-talk, and it is his wife who is missing. Why don't you stop talking and let him ask questions?'

But impatient as he was to get down to concrete facts, Howard knew that he was into a good seam here, and that it might be most productive if he simply let the stories flow. Sometimes when you tried to direct people's minds, you inadvertently steered them away from the very revelations you were hoping for.

'Of course you must realize, Sergeant, that we are being most unfair. You must think us a mad couple. But you see, we think we are living in a mad world. If you had spent a lifetime trying to see reason in political economy, you might possibly arrive at the same stage yourself. So we do tend to while away our solitude by abnegating reality. We take innocent happenings and develop the possibilities that they are not as innocent as they look. It hardly seems the sort of evidence that a high-powered modern policeman would set much store by. But you are welcome to anything we can tell you, if you think your sanity can stand up to it.'

'Just think, Walter,' his wife said. 'Some of the stories we've been concocting have got into somebody else's recurring dream. Now that might be something to work on.'

This encounter might have its potential, but it was one that could easily get out of hand. Howard felt he had to bring things down to a mundane level.

'Actually,' he said, 'we're working to the belief that it's not so much a recurring dream as an isolated memory: something from my wife's girlhood experience that she cannot connect with anything else.'

'Ah.'

Set deep in his ancient face, the professor's eyes were alive with activity.

'As if she had been here before—say when she was two to three years old.'

'Ah.'

'Could she perhaps have been incarcerated over there?'

He glanced over at the timber-framed house, whose façade somehow gave the impression of being completely deserted.

'Ah.'

This time there was a joyousness in the syllable, as if something vital had connected in the professor's mind.

'Well, not exactly incarcerated,' he said. 'And not over there. *Here*, perhaps—in *this* house—'

Well, that was even nearer to possibility. It was, after all, from this address that Jean Cossey had written to the estate agent in Broadstairs.

'So this must be one of the Agnews' stories in which there clearly must have been some element of truth. Well—there was an *element* of truth in all their stories. I think you had better tell the Sergeant this one, my dear. You have had some experience in telling it to people.'

'If you really think it's relevant—'

'How will he know whether it's relevant or not, until he's heard it? He can easily tell you to shut up—can't you, Sergeant?'

'It sounds relevant,' Howard said.

'Well—this was some years ago.'

'It is some years since my wife was three years old.'

'I can't tell you to the year when this happened. As raconteurs, the Agnews did not worry overmuch about precision. But they did know how to set a scene. They were only a rustic couple, you understand—but they had something of the talents of a Hitchcock—and one night there was a Hitchcockish arrival at their back door: black rain falling, the shutters clapping loose, the shadows Stygian—all the trappings. A young woman was tapping furtively on the door—very furtively.'

If this had not been leading so cliff-hangingly to Jean Cossey and Anne, it would have been a good story to listen to. As a story-teller, Mrs Fynes-Pym was not without finesse, and she was thoroughly enjoying herself.

'Very furtively. A young woman who certainly looked too young to own the child she was carrying in her arms. She had come, it seemed, from somewhere near Spalding—that must have been all of eight miles on the filthiest of nights. The woman was married to an American airman—they still had a base or two in Lincolnshire in those days. But it had been one of those marriages where the veneer of glamour was worn very thin. The man had turned out to be the coarsest of country hicks. He got drunk at stag parties, he knocked the pair of them about, so she was at last on the run from him, terrified about what he might do if he caught them. She begged the Agnews for shelter, just for a few days, while she got in touch through the post with friends who would help her. She had money about her and made an offer for board and lodging that was very generous indeed. Mrs Agnew would not accept more than half of it.

'The Agnews were most impressed by the child. She was quiet, intelligent—in fact to hear the old woman tell the story, you'd have thought she was a candidate for canonization. And the young woman did more than her share of the housework, but her nervousness was extreme. She was bitterly afraid that some outsider might catch sight of her. The little girl was never allowed outside, and even in the cottage she had to remember to stay well back from the window: it must have been a dreadful time for her. And the pair stayed a lot longer than the woman had first suggested they might. Then at last a letter arrived for her, and Mrs Agnew could not tell us exactly what was in it: but it was an occasion for great joy.

'They made their escape with melodramatic secrecy, very early one morning, hidden away in the back of a tradesman's van—a mobile grocery, to be exact. You can imagine, can't you, the euphoria of the Agnews, actually to be participating in an escapade like that? Mrs Agnew, of course, had put herself in charge of all the cloak and dagger trimmings.'

'Was there any later correspondence between Mrs Agnew and this woman?'

'None at all. Never a word. Mrs Agnew was very hurt by that.'

But Howard could understand it. Jean Cossey was a shrewd woman. Rural postmen were not always the best guardians of what they deduced from postmarks. Jean Cossey would not want any inkling of her whereabouts to become known in Spurlsby Drove. She would not even want Spurlsby Drove to be reminded unnecessarily of her existence.

'And she had never given the Agnews a hint as to where she was going?'

'Not the shadow of a hint.'

'I mustn't jump too readily to conclusions,' Howard said, 'just because they fit in too readily with what I'd like to think. But what if it was not from Spalding that this young woman was expecting trouble? What if it was only from the other side of the Drove? Suppose it was from the safe house she'd escaped? Would that bring in any inconsistencies?'

'It would make sense to me,' the professor said. 'Isn't it a classical truth, Sergeant, a cliché, that the best place to hide anything is almost in full view? There might have been very good reasons why the young woman did not want to travel farther than this. The weather was filthy, for one thing. For another, it's flat open country—not the sort of landscape you'd be keen to cross with a toddler if there were spiteful people after you. You'd make a sharp dash for the nearest haven—and stay there. Oh yes—I can see that.'

He actually rubbed his hands together with delight.

'Well, I thank you,' Howard said. 'And if anyone asks, I came here to consult your opinions on electoral reform. I think I'll just pop over and see if the Stablefords have any useful views on the subject.'

CHAPTER 22

His first approach to the Tudor house had been along the best training-school lines of Indian scout. Now he came openly, unworried by the crunch of his feet on the white gravel of the drive. A postal packet, too thick to go easily through the letter-box, had been jammed half into it. The ground-floor windows looked blankly at him, as if announcing unequivocally that the house was unoccupied. A cat came wandering from the back of the house, mewing piteously because it had not been fed that morning.

He went up and looked closely through a window, saw a cosy interior, a worn and clearly loved cottage living-room, such as one could easily associate with the sort of good-life people that Fynes-Pym had depicted. But here was the same sense of regimentation that he had noticed about the grounds. The neighbouring ground-floor room, on the other hand, was quite different. The furniture was modern— Swedish chairs and table in varnished pine, a music centre of Japanese manufacture, with a stack of control panels in shining metal. There was no regimentation here—rather a sense of *laissez-faire*: magazines—*Playboy* and soft porn—cast aside and left lying where they landed. There were paperbacks on the window-sill: John D. MacDonald, Ed McBain, Wilbur Smith.

Howard went to the back of the house. A gander came at him hissing. A horse's head appeared over a gate, inviting him to make friends. He looked in at the kitchen: clinically clean, with blue and white vinyl flooring. He looked up at the upstairs windows, saw that one of them had fitted bars—as one might, for instance, protect an adventurous child.

He looked over his shoulders in every direction. At this moment the premises were certainly deserted, but there was no guarantee that someone might not appear at any moment. He reflected—not for more than seconds. He had to throw all professional propriety to the winds: the consequences as far as the Force was concerned did not have to matter to him. There was one thing about outlawing oneself: one gained mightily in freedom—for the time being.

He went into such of the sheds as were not locked, looking for something with which he could climb up to look in at the barred window. He did not find a ladder—they were not going to make that kind of blunder—but he did manage to put together a combination of an old table and two barrels, together tall enough for him to get his head above the level of the sill. He looked in at a bedroom that someone had evidently left without time to put things in order. The bed had been slept in, but not remade. A plastic curtain had been drawn back in front of a washbasin alcove. There was a goodly array of toilet stuff, talcs and nail varnish, hair lacquer and cologne. The toothpaste had been left with its screw-top off. But there was nothing that he could recognize specifically as Anne's. There was a nightdress crumpled at the foot of the bed, but it was not one that he remembered ever having seen her wearing. There was a slip lying over a chair, actually hers—but he did not know that.

He climbed down, put the components of his pyramid back where he had found them and stood for a few moments in the middle of the yard as if willing some helpful clue to emerge. There was nothing he could see that told him anything.

Then he heard the creak of the front gate at the other side of the house, and the confident tread of feet on the gravel. He waited. Perhaps it was someone who would knock or ring, wait, look in and go away again. If it was someone who belonged to the house, and he was discovered here, then he would have to play it as it came.

He heard door-chimes sound somewhere indoors—so it wasn't a resident. He could picture the caller doing what he himself had done, looking in at each window before coming round the back. He heard the gander hiss and the horse try again to make a new friend. And indeed, this man did stop to fraternize briefly with the animal. Howard stood still where he was, facing the way the stranger would come. But it was not a stranger. It was Professor Fynes-Pym.

'Ah, Sergeant: you're still here. I hoped you would be. If you'll come back to the cottage, there's someone I'd like you to meet.'

Parked outside the cottage was the most disreputable old green van that Howard thought he had ever seen. Sitting at the kitchen table, talking to Mrs Fynes-Pym over an enamel mug of tea, was a man of indeterminate age whose clothing matched his transport.

'Meet Michael Osgothorpe, mole-catcher.'

And Mr Osgothorpe spoke a word or two in a language that Howard presumed to be a local variant of English.

'Mike was along this way, a few mornings ago, weren't you, Mike?'

The man nodded: a friendly informer.

'Tell Mr Lawson what you saw.'

The mole-catcher did, his enunciation not helped by the facts of being without teeth and having a mouthful of tea. Mrs Fynes-Pym laughed.

'Shall I translate?'

'Please.'

What Mr Osgothorpe had seen had been a car that fitted beautifully with the description of the one that had been parked in the forecourt of Shortlands railway station in Kent. The car had stopped a few yards after entering the Drove—

Osgothorpe's van had been parked out of sight just inside a
field-gate. The activity in which he had been involved that
morning—concerned with creatures other than moles—had
been something that he had no wish draw to the attention of
the public.

The car had stopped, and a young lady had been helped
out to be sick on the grass verge. He gave a description of her
that really was not helpful at all. But he had been able to keep
her in view until she had been assisted, walking very un-
certainly, into the house.

Howard asked to use the professor's phone. It was a relief
to get a direct line to Shiner.

CHAPTER 23

Another who did not in the least care whether he was
breaking rules, disobeying lawful commands or risking disci-
pline was Kenworthy. He again approached Swannee
Foster's property by his private road across the downs, and
this led him into an altercation with a horsey security
watcher from neighbouring territory, who suspected him
of taking a devious interest in early morning performances.
Kenworthy drove on, making no attempt to identify himself.

It was early, still wanting minutes to seven. Kenworthy
assumed that Swannee Foster was an early riser: most things
about Swannee suggested self-discipline. But Kenworthy did
not care whether the champion forger was up or not. He was
going to disturb Swannee in other ways than getting him out
of bed. He pulled up in Swannee's yard, which looked very
like any other complex of stables. And there was something
about the yard that was not quite as it should be. There was
nothing supernatural about the policeman's sense that told
Kenworthy that. For many years he had been drawing
conclusions from the lie of things, and the process of mind

had become such a habit that he sometimes came to the final answer without consciously analysing the underlying pattern.

He did not stop to analyse the pattern now. There was a silence about the place, a lack of activity that was unexpected. But maybe there would not be much activity about Swannee's yard at this hour of the morning. Swannee lived the life of a relative recluse, wasn't married, didn't have women here. But he did keep—apart from a handful of inscrutable stable-hands—a servant, a taciturn male a few years older than himself, a sort of combination of handyman, cook, gardener, ostensibly a trainer of horses and, Kenworthy suspected, what is sometimes known as a research assistant. Kenworthy did not know what arrangements Swannee and this Broadbent had, but he did rather expect Broadbent to be about and doing things at this hour. And Broadbent wasn't. Kenworthy had approached by the back of the house because he thought he might see more things of interest that way. He was curious to know, for example, what presses Swannee might have on his premises. And indeed he saw now, in what might have been taken for an ordinary tack-room, a very efficient-looking offset litho, bearing the metal plate of its Heidelberg manufacturer. He came to a door that led into the kitchen and tried the handle. It was locked, and the bellpush beside it did not look as if it were intended to be used. The button was permanently depressed and had been stuck down by a careless housepainter years ago.

The lock gave Kenworthy no difficulty. It might have done, for the skeleton keys that he carried on his ring were by no means a comprehensive collection. But the man from whom he had taken a lesson, after helping him to compose a statement, had taught him some elementary improvisations. But what Kenworthy did next was not so clever. After fumbling with the tumblers, he set his foot on a doormat that set off a burglar alarm of a primitive, quite obsolete type—

simply a set of loud bells that set up a racket all over the house. The odd thing was that this barbarous noise did not evoke any response. But the thought did not remain odd for very long. Kenworthy believed he now knew what he was likely to find when he penetrated into the living quarters; and he now believed he knew what was wrong with the pattern in the yard.

Where simple pressure on a mat caused bells to ring, there must be an electric circuit to that mat. Kenworthy stooped, raised a corner of it and wrenched wire away from a terminal. Silence followed, once the last echo had died—a silence in which he could hear the mechanism of an electric kitchen clock and the scraping of a rose-tendril against a window-pane.

The house was nineteenth-century, amorphous, labyrin-thine, designed without consideration for the convenience of living, working or extending hospitality. Kenworthy went from the kitchen down a long, cold, dark passage that led into the main entrance hall. Lying across an antique settle in this hall was Broadbent, very evidently dead; any head that hung downwards and sideways at that angle could only be trying to depend on a neck that was broken.

Kenworthy paid no attention whatever to the corpse. He went straight upstairs to the study. It was either there or in one of the bedrooms that he expected to find another body. And it was in the study that he did find it. Swannee Foster's head, arms and chest were spread inelegantly forward over his desk, with some congealment of blood on the hairs at the back of his head. It did not greatly matter to Kenworthy at this moment how he had been killed. The experts were to declare that it was by a blow from heavy metal against the cervical vertebrae, a good deal more power having been put behind it than is necessary to despatch a rabbit.

There was no sign that there had been any commotion. Current papers were about the room, but Swannee had been a moderately tidy man, and his possessions were moderately tidy. The murderer had not come here out of any interest in Swannee's belongings; he had come here purely as a murderer.

Kenworthy, however, did take an interest in things in the room—a passing interest. He touched very few things. If this had been done by the man who he thought had done it, there would not be anything as careless as prints. But if there were any prints, they might save the prosecution from having to delve into ingenuity. The correspondence on the desk was mostly about printing. It made one wonder how much of Swannee's life had been spent on his orthodox vocation. Orthodox? The top letter was from a bibliophile: trying to trace something in Latin, medieval, printed in Leipzig. Kenworthy moved over towards the shelves: great leather-bound books, a sixteenth-century German psalter, the *Meditations* of St Bonaventura. Orthodox? How many record sales at top auctions had been Swannee's products? Was it possible to fake 'early' printing, to age paper, ink and old hides? No question of it—on a level that would fool suckers. But to get past the experts? That was the whole point of Swannee's existence. It was the depth of the challenge that interested him, possibly more than the end reward. That was why, in the case of the birth certificates, he had made them mock originals.

Kenworthy's eyes wandered along the shelves, and one title that he saw there had him reaching for it. Booth: *Four Marys*. It was a fine piece of book production, a limited edition, twenty only, numbered, printed on hand-woven paper, in a type with an outlandish name: by a firm that was another name for Swannee. Author's vanity—even in the days before Edwin Booth's reputation still had to be inflated. It was well known that he had not published in the normal way, hawking his typescripts from house to house. He had gambled with his wife's capital to produce and promote himself. And Kenworthy now knew that Swannee Foster had been his printer. That explained things. It explained a lot of things. It explained why Angela and Jean Cossey had visited the downs on the day that Jean's parents came to see her. There had been papers needed for the adoption of Stella Davidge's unwanted child. This also explained how Jean Cossey had known where to come for birth certificates. But what concerned Kenworthy more at this moment was the knowledge that there had been dealings between Basset and Swannee—and between Swannee and Booth—*before* the kidnapping. Things were falling into place.

Kenworthy looked thoughtfully at the telephone, wrapped it loosely in a handkerchief and dialled with a pencil. Like Howard Lawson, he did not hesitate to beard the lion. He insisted on being put through to Cawthorne, wherever he might be, and he offered no explanation for being where he was. It was now seven-thirty. Cawthorne was shaving. He took in what Kenworthy told him, and did not find it necessary to ask any questions.

Kenworthy let himself out of the house by the way that he had come in. He looked again round the yard: a new dent in a dustbin, the handle of a bass broom snapped along its short grain, where a wheel had run over it, tyre-marks reversing up to a stable-door at one angle, then out again at another. Someone had tried to do a three-point turn, unaccustomed to the confinement and the geometry: someone who had been in a hurry, in the dark—perhaps not entirely his normal self.

Kenworthy drove down towards the public highways of Royal Berkshire. Again a tweedy trainer's strong-arm resented the intrusion. This time he was determined to make a job's worth of trouble, stood in the path of the oncoming Kenworthy waving his arms. Kenworthy showed him his warrant card through the window.

'Why didn't you say so?'

'Too much of a hurry. You'll know why in the next news bulletin but one. Have you been on watch all night?'

'Since first light.'

'Anyone else come this way?'

A three-litre Merc, maroon with dove-grey trim. Driver was a big man, cross between a gorilla and a grizzly. The stable-guard had thought he was going to run him down.

Kenworthy stopped to phone again in the next village. Cawthorne was racing through his breakfast.

CHAPTER 24

The jolting of tyres over the ruts in Spurlsby Drove; the marginally better surface of a flinty lane. Then came sleeping villages, humpy bridges over fenland drains, and at last a long straight road westwards towards the A1.

Anne had screamed at the moment when it had looked as if there was no stopping Basset. And Basset, clamping a sweat-salty, nicotine-stained hand over her mouth, had laughed at her, slapping his other hand over her breast and shoving her towards the bed.

But feet raced up the stairs.

'Stop it, you bloody fool!'

Basset let Anne go—he really was quite drunk. Angela looked at him contemptuously, said nothing more, showed no sympathy for Anne.

'She was getting out of hand,' Basset said.

Anne had scratched his face badly. It satisfied her to see the blood running down past the corners of his mouth. Angela was looking at him as if she considered him a pathetic object. Then her forearm swept and her knuckles cracked down across his mouth, knocking him back against the washbasin.

'I told you to lay off the booze. Put your head under the cold tap. Sober yourself. Big Daddy's phoned. He'll see us tonight.'

She turned to Anne.

'Get yourself ready for the road. I can lend you an outdoor coat.'

Angela drove. Basset, slumped on the rear seat with Anne, smelt offensively of liquor, but mercifully could not keep awake. Anne tried at first to keep track of the crossings and turnings, but within a quarter of an hour all sense of direction had deserted her.

'I didn't think your Papa would agree without more fuss than this. Mind you, he knows it's a little bit more than a family reunion. He knows what publicity could do for him. Still, the battle's not on yet. We haven't even drawn swords. And he'll still have to be convinced. You've had no more ideas, I suppose?'

'Not a thing.'

And she did not want to. Anne could hear Angela's voice, but she was barely listening to it. She was weighing up the sense of making a dash for it, if they stopped anywhere. With Basset in stupefied sleep, it would only be between her and Angela. There were bound to be moments when Angela's attention was divided. But she had to remember that Angela might be armed. She was quite likely to be carrying a miniature pistol about her somewhere.

Did she not want to meet her father? Did she believe now that Edwin Booth was her father? Yes and no. She supposed so, though the blue-bird was still the only positive evidence—except that there were scars of a sort under her shoulder-blade—visible if you were looking for them. The reality was too remote to mean much to her: as remote as the thought that if all Angela said was true, she might become a rich woman. Was it priggish to say that the money did not interest her? Well, if money was her due, why did she need Angela and Basset to claim it for her? The pair were going into this as if it were a new crime they were committing. It *was* a crime, anyway: there was a strong stink of blackmail about it. And it was in the course of these machinations that someone, someone who was in this with Basset and Angela, had foully killed Jean Cossey. How many people were in on this?

'You nearly spilled the beans once, you little brat, saying you saw Edwin come out of my room in his bathrobe. That's something you might remind him of.'

Basset belched and slobbered in his sleep. They were quite likely to have to stop in a lay-by for him. She might be able to slip away into darkness, make her way to a phone.

'Another time, Edwin and I were desperately trying to get you to occupy yourself for ten minutes. But would you turn your eyes the other way? In the garden of a pub at Shillingford Bridge, that was. You might try that one on him.'

'He'd know you've been coaching me.'

'Listen, you stupid little bitch, do you know how much depends on how you play this? If you go and goof it up—'

Basset lurched over sideways, his full weight across her right arm. She levered him off and he fell forward against the back of Angela's head.

'Angela, can't I for God's sake come and sit in front? And let this lump have the seat to himself?'

'Makes sense. If I can find somewhere to pull up discreetly.'

That would be her chance.

'We are not amused, Kenworthy. It is not amusing. We have work to do, and your troubles must wait. But you're going to receive a ripe old panful from a high altitude this time.'

Cawthorne's inner office: they were waiting for Wright and Lawson to join them.

'Swannee wanted you off his back because he knew they'd kill him if you showed any more open interest.'

'Why didn't you tell me that?'

'You know what clout Swannee had in some quarters.'

'Because he had provided forged documentation in his time—that had had people sent down?'

'Not in any case of mine if that's what you're thinking,'
Cawthorne said.

When the other two arrived together, Lawson was looking
all in. Wright was merely dog-tired.

'Right, let's have it, Sergeant. Quickly and without frills.
What did you find in Lincolnshire? And never mind what
you were doing there. That will come later.'

Lawson gave it them in a dozen sentences.

'Now put Wright in the picture about Swannee, Simon.'

Kenworthy was even more succinct.

'It's like doing a jigsaw-puzzle picture side down,'
Cawthorne said. 'So now let's have your theory.'

'Booth and Swannee were in cahoots eighteen years ago.
They had a business relationship—Swannee was printing
Booth's books. Booth wanted rid of his wife and daughter
and thought up a scheme to get them killed on a kidnap
retrieval that went wrong. He couldn't mount it himself,
because he hadn't the contacts. Swannee had the contacts,
but wouldn't look at that sort of caper unless the lolly was
abundant. Booth was one of the few men in the country who
could talk the sort of money that Swannee would look at. So
Swannee put himself under contract, recruited Len Basset to
do the close-quarter work—Basset was an up-and-coming
post-war hoodlum who didn't draw the line at anything he
was being paid enough for. He also had a small string on the
streets that Angela—the Davidge girl—had just joined. The
very woman to bring in as nursemaid: leave her references to
Swannee. Then there was Jean Cossey, naive, sentimental
and good-hearted—the very one to mind the child during
phase one. They were paid one third to a half of their fees in
advance: that's standard practice—and that's where Jean's
Egbert came from. The kidnapping took place. The killings
were scheduled for the hand-over. Jean and the child were
shunted into one of Swannee's long-term sidings, the safe
house in Lincolnshire where Stableford was caretaker.'

Cawthorne had started taking notes at first, but was now

drawing arabesques on his pad.

'Jean took the child—as she was bound to, being Jean—
and she may have had a brainstorm, or she may have
overheard something. At any rate, she got to know what the
next stage in the plan was: there was going to be shooting at
the rendezvous that Basset was going to set up. We know
what happened: Diane Booth fatally shot. But Anne had
been saved by Jean Cossey. We don't know the details. We
probably never shall, with Jean Cossey dead and Anne too
young to remember. But somehow Jean got Anne out of that
safe house, even though she had neither the time nor the
energy to get her farther than across the road. And Swannee
did a double cover-up. He had Basset impersonated in
County Durham, and at the same time had it slipped to Sid
Heather that the word among the mushes was that Basset
had had the biggest finger in the Booth pie.'

Cawthorne had now completed a Moorish frieze down one
side of his paper.

'Basset did his spell for holding up the post-office he'd
been nowhere near. When he got out, he got somehow on the
trail of Jean Cossey in Broadstairs. It wouldn't surprise me if
it was Angela who'd traced her, and was waiting for him to
come out and do the rough stuff. He met the pair at the
kindergarten gate and demanded hush money. That was
why there was a big withdrawal from one of her building
society accounts just before she went up north. You drew
attention to that, very early on, Shiner. Why was she parting
with a thousand at the very time when she could least afford
to? It had to be because she was terrified of Mr Camel-
Leopard—Basset. It was a crafty move, vanishing into working Lancashire the way she did. It was so unlikely—as
unlikely as hiding in Waterman's Cottage. There were
times when I'd take my hat off to Jean Cossey—if only she
could have been consistent. She had the nerve—and the
stupidity—to run away from Lancashire in the first place
to try to become a groupie. And if you ask me, she never

had wholly grown away from the kid she'd been in those days.'

Cawthorne had started on a sea-serpent, each coil with its circle of ripples in the waves.

'We don't know yet—maybe we can ask them—why they left it so long before trying to see what more they could screw out of Booth. There may have been a bit of publicity about Anne's forthcoming wedding—an engagement party photograph in the local press—something like that. It got somebody talking—and thinking. Swannee must have been in on it, otherwise they wouldn't have had the use of his place up in Lincs. And if Swannee was in on it, that means he was in charge. He'd never have taken orders from Basset. And I don't think the main thrust was to sell Anne back to her father. I think they meant to blackmail him for the whole thing—for commissioning the kidnapping, for what can be charged as the murder of his wife. They couldn't, of course, have shopped him to us. But the threat of memoirs in the press would have left him little choice. To sell it in Fleet Street, they'd have to muster every shred of evidence that they could show: Anne and Jean Cossey too. We don't know yet who killed Jean. Not Booth, because he hadn't been brought into the act at that stage. I'm certain that Angela was involved—because of that Lewisham alibi. Why else should she need an alibi? And my guess is that Basset was with her—at least in the final stages. Jean Cossey was in an alcoholic stupor. She had to be undressed and carried into the bathroom. The ramshackle electrics had to be rigged. Angela might feasibly have managed it all alone. I don't think she'd have cared to—but with assistance it would have been relatively easy.'

'But why kill Jean Cossey?'

'There's surely only one reason for that—because, perhaps to their surprise, she wouldn't play. What did they need her for? As additional proof of Anne's identity. Especially since she was the one who could speak authoritatively of what sort of a child Anne had been in those days—what were her whims and fancies—what were her real feelings about her parents. Remember that Anne would have talked to Jean as she had never talked to Angela. Jean's information was crucial if Booth was to be convinced that this really was Anne. Angela and Basset may have been surprised that Jean didn't want to be cut in on the final act. Who wouldn't want to be cut in for that sort of money? Short answer: Jean Cossey—because Jean Cossey had suffered all her life from a sentimental sense of honour. She knew where Anne's happiness lay—in being happily married to a detective-sergeant. Jean Cossey's heart was never anywhere but in the right place. But all her life she had had the unfortunate defect of not being able to see round more than three out of every four corners. She may not actually have threatened to blow the gaffe. But she may have given her thoughts away to the point at which she had them worried.'

'And nobody foresaw that Booth might want to settle this bit of bother in his own way.'

'That's my reading. Booth's a big man. He thinks big and he acts big. And the risk's worth it, because the price he'd have to pay would be too steep. And there was no compromise in the way he disposed of Swannee and Broadbent.'

'So where are they taking Anne?'

'To meet her father, I think. He'll have made an appointment. He'll have told them he's ready to do a deal. And remember, Angela and Basset haven't got Swannee's subtle direction now. I don't need to tell you that Anne is in a very dangerous position.'

Wright leaned forward to the Commander. 'You're still tracing Booth's course, sir?'

'We are tracing the courses of three men who could be Booth. Booth has money for everything, and he didn't have to go to Swannee for a heavy mob this time. Let's go to the Control Room.'

CHAPTER 25

It was one of those lay-bys that used to be a loop in the road, leafy, undulant and blind. Angela had misjudged the distance from the blue *Parking* sign and pulled into it late and roughly. Basset was thrown almost off the seat, but the jolt did not wake him. Angela switched off the engine, sat for a moment savouring the silence, then got out to come round to the passenger side. She opened Anne's door.

'I don't know what we're going to do with this bugger. He's going to be in no fit state for Edwin Booth to see.'

Anne stepped out into the night. A patch of illumination from the courtesy light fell on the deteriorated tarmac. The headlamps were dipped and playing on to a rubbish receptacle that had not been emptied for many months. It was remarkable what people found to throw away in lay-bys.

'We'll have to leave him out of negotiations,' Angela said. 'Things can't go any more awry for that.'

'Does he often get into this state?' Anne asked her. But that proved to have been the wrong thing to say.

'Listen, kid. Don't get up-market about Len. You've not learned enough in your young life to know what's what between women and men. We don't all go for the CID. OK—get in. We've a good two hours' drive yet. I'd like to find a hotel somewhere where we can freshen up a bit.'

'Where are we meeting my father?'

To have called him Mr Booth would have sounded fatuous, but the word *father* came unnaturally to her lips.

'No questions. Let's keep things the way they've been. Neither of us has made any bad mistakes up to now.'

And that was an answer to a question more important than the one she had actually asked. Although there was an uneasy appearance of trust between them, and although it was nominally as allies that they were calling on Edwin Booth, Angela was still the watch-dog. Split-second timing was needed now—the moment before Anne got back into the car was vital. Angela's fingers were on the button of the doorhandle. She was putting out her other hand to push Anne's arm. And they both heard another car coming along the road from the direction in which they had come themselves. It did not dip its headlights as it came to rest some ten yards behind them and Angela, momentarily dazzled, turned her eyes aside.

It was Anne's chance to sidestep. She had already spotted the pocket of black shadow into which she intended to dodge, hoping then to impede pursuit by zigzagging tactics. Angela clawed out for her, but missed her by the vital inch. Anne took a step backwards, crossed the tarmac, darted forward, turned back towards the main road, came back on her footsteps and was almost abreast of the car again as Angela was running from it.

And that was the stage they had reached when another car passed the entrance to the lay-by. It slowed down, its power smoothly restrained—and turned in at the further entrance to the loop.

Cawthorne looked proudly down at his beflagged operational map. It did not look as if there were any area of the kingdom in which he was not deploying someone—or persuading himself that he was.

'There's one who crossed southern England to go to Dieppe. I have to admit he's foxed us. There's one who came over at Southampton, and I'll swear that's Booth. And there are any number of other reports, most of which just have to be false—and every one of which has been followed up. There's one in Nottinghamshire that I don't believe for a moment, but there's a tail on him all the same.'

'Notts isn't all that far from Lincs, sir,' Lawson muttered.

'We'll soon know. The orders are clear: not to lose sight of their quarry at any price, but to give him as long a leash as safety will allow. The object has been, you see, gentlemen, to see where these fellows will lead us.'

He looked round their faces to see whether this lesson in subtle strategy from high level experience was being appreciated.

'And until now, we had no reason to believe that Edwin Booth had himself committed any crime.'

'We don't disbelieve it now, I hope,' Kenworthy said.

'We don't disbelieve it now. So now we start pulling them all in—wherever each of them happens to be at this precise moment.'

He went and gave a brief instruction to the uniformed inspector in technical charge of his battle-room. His action orders were carried down on an endless belt to the telephonists who would relay them out to the teams.

Radio waves carried the messages out into the night. A bear-like man in a motel in Oxfordshire was dragged out of the bed which he was sharing with a woman whom he had not set eyes on four hours previously. Another putative Booth was at a hotel in Basingstoke—alone in a single room, and it took time to establish that he had no connection at all with the affair in hand. Another innocent, who had had a double tail on him for days, was in a twin-bedded room with his wife at their home in Bracknell. None of these was Edwin Booth; but the characters in Basingstoke and Oxfordshire were held on suspicion of being his associates—a fact eventually proven in one of their cases.

Cawthorne's action order reached the couple who were following the real Edwin Booth just before Angela turned into the lay-by for Anne to change seats. They had not been aware of Anne and Angela, who had been ahead of Booth throughout the night's drive. With two colleagues alternating in another car, they had been trailing Booth for forty-eight hours, overnighting close to him in Maidstone, Tonbridge and Norwich. It seemed an odd route that he was following, and his behaviour was that of a casual and very arbitrary tourist. He looked at a parish church here, an ancient market-hall there. In Norwich he appeared to have settled down for the night, and the quartet had decided to make a dog-watch of it. Then he had reappeared just before midnight and made his way down to the hotel car park.

First he drove south-west, gave London a wide western berth, and went up into the hills above Newbury along a private road on which they could not follow him without drawing fatal attention to themselves. He was not out of their ken for more than an hour, and spent the inside of that day in Windsor. It was only after his evening meal that he moved north again, making for King's Lynn and then up along the east coast route. Finally he had turned west again, as if to cross the backbone of the country. He was driving fast, but always within the legal limits: a man not wanting to risk embroilment that might draw attention to himself.

His tail almost missed his turn into the lay-by. But by now they were absolutely convinced that of all Cawthorne's mobiles, they were the ones who were on to the real thing. They reported this conviction over their radio net, and were reminded to stick strictly to orders. That was at 1.20 a.m. At 1.42 they were told, as were their colleagues everywhere else, to intercept their prey as immediately as was feasible. They cruised past the lay-by and turned into its second entry just as Anne was getting out of the car. And they saw Booth, who was now getting out of his: holding a hand-gun.

The policemen were not armed. It was no time for heroics that could easily have put an end to their own existence, and would probably have been lethal for the women. One of them stayed in the car long enough to radio to their leap-frogging oppos, calling for urgent support. This pair were less than three-quarters of a mile behind.

They saw Anne dart away towards the main road and lost sight of her. Then Angela saw that Booth was taking aim at her, and she screamed. Anne went unattended to for an instant.

'We are police officers,' one of the constables shouted from the shadows. 'Drop your gun.'

Booth fired at where he judged the voice to have come from. Then he fired at Angela, and missed her as she spurted for shadow. Then Booth turned sideways with a yelp. Something had hit him hard on the side of his head: a half-brick thrown by Anne from close range.

Then the second police car was arriving, very fast along the main road, disconcertingly noisy and throwing a great deal of light over the arena. The two officers who had been first on the scene rushed Booth simultaneously, from different angles. He was bulky, powerful and desperate, giving the pair of them a memorable fight, even after his weapon had been knocked from his hand. But he was no match for four young fighters, although there was a good deal of bruising and abrasion and considerable damage to uniform. They overpowered him in the end, and then it took time for them to be convinced of Anne's identity. They consulted each other about Basset, and it was decided that one of them should drive him in his own car to the nearest police station. Throughout the skirmish he had come to no kind of coherent consciousness.

For the rest of the night they lost Angela. But Cawthorne had enough patrols within a ten-mile radius of that lay-by to have guaranteed the security of a foreign head of state. She was picked up in the early grey of morning, trying to hitch a lift.

There were loose ends to be got into comprehensible order. Angela was confronted by the officers who had reported her for a traffic transgression in Lewisham. She insisted for some hours that she was not the woman they had dealt with—until they got her so weary that she started tripping into inconsistencies.

Even then she might have beaten them over the main

issue, had they not been holding Basset in a different part of the building. Like most professionals played one against the other, they were blasé at first about the insinuations about betrayals going on behind their backs. But they were up against experts who knew how to let doubts creep in—and how to make the most of it when the veneers began to crack.

Basset was the first to weaken. They had worked on him overnight before they struck oil by telling him that Angela had admitted that they had met Jean Cossey in a pub a couple of hours before the murder.

'And a right state she was in,' Basset said. 'She never had been able to hold her drink. She was always ready to pass out after three or four. Angela took her home to her flat. How am I to know what happened when she got her there?'

They got the name of the pub out of him; they found witnesses from both sides of the bar; they gave Angela Basset's written statement to read.

They knew she would not let Basset leave her facing it alone. She agreed that they had met Jean Cossey by arrangement. It was true that Jean had had a drop too much—but that did not mean much in her case. Angela had got her home before it became a case of having to carry her there. And, yes, they'd had another drink or two on arrival. Basset had followed an hour later. Angela was too tough to be pushed nearer an admission than that; but the jury were perceptive.

Angela Hallam was not known in the archives under that name, but under others she was on record: with her prints. It was the dates of her previous offences that were interesting.

She had spent some months on remand in custody very shortly after the kidnapping, having overstretched herself while Basset was in gaol for the post-office job. She had battened on to an itinerant executive, who had thrown a surprise by having her brought in for fraudulent pretences. And it was when she was free again—some time after Basset reappeared—that he had travelled to Broadstairs to become known as Mr Camel-Leopard. A few years later she had received a substantial custodial sentence. She had been recruiting for Basset—and others—adolescent girls who were still getting themselves stranded in London in their hundreds. It was not known how Jean Cossey got to hear of that—she could have read it in the papers; what was significant was that that was the time that she had judged it safe to re-emerge from Slodden-le-Woods.

It was a curious situation. Basset had saved her from being Stella Davidge, not by taking her off the streets, but by putting her on them. But things had not taken long to change. Admittedly, the biggest crime had been at Edwin Booth's instigation, but Swannee Foster had been the entrepreneur who had got things moving for him, and it was Angela who had ended up in command of Basset. The judge had some old-fashioned and hurtful things to say when he passed a life-sentence on the pair of them for the murder of Jean Cossey.

Booth was tried separately. His counsel made as much as he could of the prejudicial effect that the trial of Angela and Basset must have had on the minds of the jury. He had to: it was one of the few arguable points that he could spin time from.

He was overruled. In his charge to the jurors, the judge told them that they must put out of their minds anything they had heard about the case anywhere but in that court-room.

No one believed that they would or could—or that it would make an atom of difference. The identification of Booth by a stable security guard was one of those balance-tipping sensations that hit the headlines from time to time.

Angela and Basset, handcuffed to escorts, were rigorously kept out of sight of each other in the interval between giving their evidence—in which they disagreed in detail here and there: but not in direct incrimination of Booth.

Another life sentence—with one of those sour, mouth-downward-turning declarations from the Bench that he should serve at least twenty years. That would give him very little borrowed time to play with on his release.

Anne was allowed ten minutes with him in a cell under the court before they took him away. It was a meeting that she mentally refused to face up to until the final moment. She could have no love for him—only a curiosity so repellent that she could only regard it as an obscenity.

There was no rapport between them. Booth was as inarticulate as she was. He murmured something about at least not being a poor man, and he would see that she was recompensed. This seemed an even greater obscenity. It was remarkable—though no one who mattered remarked upon it—how closely the real facts had followed the theories that Kenworthy had propounded in Cawthorne's office. There was one aspect that he had not been able to get right, and this was cleared up when a couple called Stableford were picked up close to Spalding. The Stablefords were principally smallholders, but he had been warden of Foster's house in Spurlsby Drove for many years. He proclaimed that he did not know of many of the things that had gone on there, and in that he was probably telling largely the truth, for it would have suited Swannee to keep him ignorant. He had taken his wife away from the house the morning after Basset and Angela had left—but that was mainly to avoid questioning. And he did not go far. His gardening and caretaking were better than his criminal tactics. And he was able to shed a little light on Jean Cossey. It was during the shoot-out after the kidnapping that Jean had managed to save Anne's life—simply by making sure that she was nowhere near the place where she had been told to keep her. Blood was found on the grass, it was true, but this was from no more than a cut produced in a tumble. And in that tumble they were recaptured by one of Basset's mobsters, who drove them fast back to Lincolnshire to await Basset's orders. It was then that Jean gave them the slip by a trick—and crossed the Drove.

★

Was it to be Brighton? Frinton? Felixstowe? It had crossed Howard Lawson's mind that there might be some therapy in Broadstairs—but he had dismissed the thought before suggesting it. It wasn't that they would not be able to go to the Costa del Sol again within the foreseeable future. The lawyers were taking their time over making over money from Booth to Anne. And Anne felt indifferent about the whole issue: but she would have something coming to her. And no disciplinary action was going to be taken against Howard—really that was because, for some reason, Cawthorne wasn't taking any against Kenworthy.

The Lawsons went for a break to Southwold, where it rained for their three days. But they enjoyed it more than they had Horley, Surrey.